PLATFORM PAPERS

QUARTERLY ESSAYS ON THE PERFORMING ARTS

No. 23
April 2010

CURRENCY HOUSE

PLATFORM PAPERS
Quarterly essays from Currency House Inc.

Editor: Dr John Golder, j.golder@unsw.edu.au

Currency House Inc. is a non-profit association and resource centre advocating the role of the performing arts in public life by research, debate and publication.

Postal address: PO Box 2270, Strawberry Hills, NSW 2012, Australia

Email: info@currencyhouse.org.au   Tel: (02) 9319 4953
Website: www.currencyhouse.org.au   Fax: (02) 9319 3649

Editorial Board: Katharine Brisbane AM, Dr John Golder, John McCallum, Martin Portus, Greig Tillotson

ISBN 978-0-9805632-7-6
ISSN 1449-583X
Typeset in 10.5 Arrus BT
Printed by Hyde Park Press, Richmond, SA
Author's photograph on cover by Brett Monaghan

This edition of Platform Papers is supported by the Keir Foundation, the Greatorex Foundation, Neil Armfield, David Marr, Joanna Murray-Smith and other individual donors and advisers. To them and to all our supporters Currency House extends sincere gratitude.

Contents

AVAILABILITY *Platform Papers*, quarterly essays on the performing arts, is published every January, April, July and October and is available through bookshops or by subscription. For order form, see page 84.

LETTERS Currency House invites readers to submit letters of 400–1,000 words in response to the essays. Letters should be emailed to the Editor at info@currencyhouse.org.au or posted to Currency House at PO Box 2270, Strawberry Hills, NSW 2012, Australia. To be considered for the next issue, the letters must be received by 10 May 2010.

CURRENCY HOUSE For membership details, see our website at: www.currencyhouse.org.au

Whatever Happened to the STC Actors Company?

JAMES WAITES

The author

James Waites is a graduate of what was at the time the School of Drama at the University of New South Wales. Initially employed by ABC radio as an arts documentary scriptwriter, he returned to UNSW as a part-time tutor and later lectured part-time at Theatre Nepean, University of Western Sydney. While a student he was invited to participate in a 10-day workshop in Armidale, NSW, with the great Polish theatre-maker, Jerzy Grotowski. In 1980, he worked as a research assistant to director Rex Cramphorn on his experimental 'A Shakespeare Company'. A few years later he joined Cramphorn again for another season of Shakespeare productions, this time at the Playbox Theatre in Melbourne.

James is probably best known as a journalist specialising in the performing arts. He came to prominence in the early 1980s, as drama critic for the highly regarded *National Times*; and was also drama critic for the *Sydney Morning Herald* for much of the 1990s. At other times he has been a regular contributor to the *Independent Monthly*, the *Sydney Review* and the *Bulletin*.

Since 1993, James has been employed as an Interviewer for the National Library of Australia's Oral History Department, where he has focused on two major projects: 'Australia's Response to AIDS' and interviews with Australia's senior theatre professionals. In recent years he has also been invited into the large, creative theatre family called Big hART, documenting process on a number of productions including the acclaimed *Ngapartji Ngapartji*. He will be engaged in a similar capacity on their co-production (with Company B) of *Namatjira*, playing at Belvoir Street Theatre in late 2010.

James has established his own website – www.jameswaites.com – where he reports on theatre activity in Sydney, among other broader themes. He shares his Surry Hills apartment with two cats, Amos and Nitro.

Acknowledgements

Who would have thought, after having experienced all ten of the stage productions created by the short-lived STC Actors Company that I would be given a chance to reconsider that experience in depth? As a regular theatregoer, I had followed the project closely, from the stalls. All the productions were 'interesting', and several I count among my favourite experiences in the theatre.

So when I was approached by Currency House to write a Platform Paper on 'the life and times', as it were, of the Actors Company, I jumped at the chance. When asked what my views were in advance, I said I had none. I had opinions on each of the productions, but as for the project overall … What views could I have? Who knows what goes on behind closed doors?

I accepted the assignment on the agreement that I would base it on interviews with key participants, chiefly the original team of actors invited to join the project, whom I have taken to calling the 'Holy Twelve'. I spoke with nine of them: Brandon Burke, Peter Carroll, Marta Dusseldorp, Eden Falk, John Gaden, Hayley McElhinney, Amber McMahon, Pamela Rabe and Dan Spielman. I also spoke with two others who joined the project later on: Ewen Leslie and Luke Mullins. Those conversations were fascinating, hugely helpful, and I thank them all for trusting me with their stories.

Other actors who featured significantly in works created by the AC are Deborah Mailman, Colin Moody and Martin Blum (foundation members); as well as Paul Capsis, Helen Thomson, Emily Russell, Robert Menzies and Steve Le Marquand. Not to forget two whole years of National Institute of Dramatic Art (NIDA) acting students.

Before speaking to any of the actors, I got to spend some time with four of the key players from AC creative management. Directors Barrie Kosky and Benedict Andrews, who happened, as luck would have it, to be in Sydney for brief periods at the right time.

Most importantly, I had a chance to speak with Robyn Nevin who, as STC Artistic Director (1999–2007), raised the funds for the project and brought it into being. This proved to be a David-and-Goliath battle, not without controversy. I want to thank Robyn Nevin for not just sharing her thoughts with me, but also for her brave, open-hearted honesty. She may be known to be tough on others at times in the making of work; let me assure you, she is much tougher on herself. I also spoke at length with her Artistic Associate, Tom Wright.

From STC staff, I also interviewed General Manager, Rob Brookman; Company Manager, Egil Kipste; and Senior Stage Manager, Georgia Gilbert. I thank them all. In total I recorded some fifty hours of conversation, from which I have distilled the key themes of this essay.

My main regret, in having to control the length of

the essay, is that I have only been able to mention in passing, or by implication, the contributions made by a number of very talented designers. To do justice to their work would require another entire publication. Let me at least mention them here by name: Ralph Myers and Robert Cousins (set design); Tess Schofield and Alice Babidge (costume design); Nick Schlieper and Damien Cooper (lighting design); Alan John and Max Lyandvert (music) and Movement Consultant Gavin Robins and Voice Coach Charmian Gradwell.

And a final 'thank you' to the indispensable Jane Seldon and Lauren Proietti, Wardrobe Supervisor and Wig and Hair Supervisor respectively, who provided pastoral care, support and practical maintenance throughout the entire Actors Company experience.

On a personal note, can I thank my best friends Maggie Blinco, Christopher Tomkinson, Augusta Supple and Jason Fuller for keeping me alive over these past few months? I love yous all!

And finally to my editor, John Golder. How the poor man has survived to tell the tale, I have no idea. Thank you so much, John. I mean it from the bottom of my heart: I could not have done it without you.

1

'Be Careful What You Pray For'

I have never been anything but a risk-taker.
I have always taken risks.

Robyn Nevin

I t was late afternoon on 10 January 2004, a perfect summer's day, when the then NSW State Premier, Bob Carr, stood up at the Wharf Restaurant to speak. This elegant room, jutting out into the blue-green waters of the Harbour, was handling a function for Sydney Theatre Company sponsors and supporters, hosted by STC Artistic Director Robyn Nevin and General Manager Rob Brookman. Visiting British playwright Tom Stoppard was a special guest. These privileged few were enjoying a dinner break between performances of two new works, *Harbour* and *The Republic of Myopia*, plays that Nevin had commissioned to inaugurate the impressive new Sydney Theatre, across the road from the STC's Wharf Theatre and Restaurant.

Earlier that same day Nevin had encountered Stoppard crossing the road between the two buildings.

'Never open a new theatre with a new show,' he admonished. 'And you are doing it with two!' Nevin was aware of the risk, but had her reasons. She knew that Carr would be present—his government had bankrolled the new auditorium—and she wanted to remind him of another important item on the company's wish-list.

The Sydney Theatre had never been Nevin's project. It was the baby of her predecessor, Wayne Harrison, who had a greater interest in musicals and other large-scale forms of popular work. Indeed, when Nevin took over the running of the STC in 1999, she immediately ordered that the interior be redesigned to better suit her primary interest in the production of classics and mainstream spoken drama.

Nevin's personal motive in opening the new theatre with two very different shows sharing one cast was to demonstrate to Bob Carr and his money people, the STC Board and the media what an 'ensemble' of actors might be capable of—a straight play followed by a musical, perhaps?—given even a sliver of a chance. To this end, she had commissioned Katherine Thomson to write *Harbour*, and Jonathan Biggins, Drew Forsythe and Phillip Scott to write *The Republic of Myopia* for the same ten actors.

Before the curtain went up on the second production, across the road at the Harbourside supper, Carr had made his historic announcement. As knives and forks fell to silence, he began: 'Robyn came to me to ask …' As she looked over to Rob Brookman, Nevin could have finished the sentence: 'Two sobs came out and I had to choke back incredible emotion. I knew what Bob was going to say.' Her long-held dream for a 'best-of-the-best', all-Australian actors' ensemble was about to come true.

When she pitched for the artistic directorship of the STC in 1999, Nevin already had the creation of such an ensemble in mind. But she had not put it into her job application, and did not mention it when interviewed. She merely said that she wanted 'a fine drama company'. Had she been asked to explain, she would have done so. To her, the STC was not a fine drama company, not yet. 'It was a company that produced projects, one after the other.' That was not fine.

Carr probably knew that he was likely to withdraw from politics soon, and his offer—funding of $2.5 million over five years for an actors' ensemble, to operate within the embrace of the larger STC—was his last major cultural gift to the city of Sydney. The proposal had been discussed for three years, from 2001 to 2003, and there had been meetings at the highest level, with the Premier's advisors, including Roger Wilkins, Director General of Arts, to consider detailed budgets and plans.

'The shape and size of the Actors Company (AC) that emerged was pretty much as per [our] submission,' says Brookman. 'We thought [$2.5 million] would be enough. It was always intended that the company would fund-raise for the balance of the cost, as it's never very appealing to a government to pick up 100 per cent of a bill.' Indeed, the company was successful in getting major sponsor Audi on board, as well as raising funds from individual donors. In rough terms, the total costs were envisaged as $700,000 per annum, with $500,000 from Government and $200,000 from corporate and private support.

Getting the AC up and running involved endeavour on many fronts: Which actors were to be involved? What would they do? How might they go about it? After the initial flush of excitement, in the sober light of the weeks that followed Carr's announcement, an awful reality sank in: the Premier's timing had been less than ideal. 'When it happened, I wasn't ready for it,' admits Nevin. 'Nor was the STC.'

The fact is, she and Brookman had 'given up on the possibility of the grant coming through' and, when the announcement came, they were in a 'total state of unreadiness'. With adequate warning they would have planned for the AC to start in 2005, but 'an announcement in January 2004 didn't leave [them] enough time to put the AC together and build it into [their] programming for the next year.' As it was, organizing for the ensemble to begin work in April 2006 proved difficult enough: 'The complexity of it all was almost unbearable,' says Nevin. 'That was a problem for me, and, I think, […] a problem from which we never recovered.' Over the early months matters only got worse.

What kind of ensemble?

By its very nature theatre is a social activity, group-created, and the best theatre strives to reflect the ideals of an ensemble approach—one in which the work that results on stage, the 'whole', if you like, is noticeably greater than the sum of its component parts. How this is best achieved has led to many variations of two basic models.

There is the 'guru' model, which, at its most intense, involves a finite group of actors with shared artistic ideals, probably on equal pay (if any at all), who create new work from the ground up under the guidance of a visionary leader. The focus of the work tends to be on process rather than product, and the results on stage are often described as 'organic' in appearance.

Jerzy Grotowski's Poland-based troupe and Peter Brook's Paris-based company of international actors, both acclaimed for an acting-focused 'poor theatre' style, are probably the most renowned of the past 50 years. Both these gurus influenced the experimental work of Rex Cramphorn, whose Performance Syndicate operated in Sydney from 1969 to 1975. Cramphorn worked with various versions of process-driven ensembles until his death in 1991, but his original group included a young Robyn Nevin.

Other Australian examples of the guru model, all Melbourne-based, include Australian Nouveau Theatre (1981–94), led by director Jean-Pierre Mignon; Gilgul Theatre Company (1990–98), led by director Barrie Kosky; the Keene/Taylor Theatre Project (1997–2002), with writer-director team, Daniel Keene and Ariette Taylor; and Ranters, with another writer-director team, Raimondo and Adriano Cortese, now in its sixteenth year of operation. Several of the AC artists had experience in one of more of these ensembles.

The other, less democratic model might be called 'institutional'. Here, enhanced artistic freedom flourishes within an often larger, more formal structure. Two of the directors who worked with the AC, Barrie Kosky and Benedict Andrews, brought experience from leading European models, the Vienna Schauspielhaus and Berlin's Schaubühne am Lehniner Platz respectively.

'Institutional' models may have a charismatic leader, but usually employ other directors; the acting ensemble is large in number (usually around 30); pay rates are scaled; and members are generally free to come and go, dropping out to make a film or dropping in for a particular role. The work, on a spectrum of priorities, is focused on 'product', on 'good results'.

The most successful of several Australian examples of this model was perhaps the Melbourne Theatre Company in the late 1960s under John Sumner, its high point being George Ogilvie's production of *The Cherry Orchard* (1969), with a full-time company of 28 actors. Known as 'an actor's director', Ogilvie also led another successful 'institutional' ensemble, the State Theatre Company of South Australia, between 1972 and 1976, of which the AC's John Gaden was a member.

Contemporaneous with Sumner's MTC, the Old Tote in Sydney deployed a similar model under the artistic directorship of Robin Lovejoy. As a NIDA student, Robyn Nevin understudied roles at the Tote, and worked there consistently for several years after graduating. Productions might have been conservative by today's tastes, but the Tote, essentially a provincial English repertory company, was well-organized, had high technical standards, and gave young actors like Nevin considerable experience.

Since the 1970s, there have been numerous (if often short-lived) attempts in Australia to upgrade the quality of acting and productions generally, within the now-established state theatre model. The most relevant to this essay—Brookman says it was actually in Nevin's mind as she put the AC together—is the State Theatre Company of South Australia under the artistic direction of Jim Sharman, renamed Lighthouse (1982–84). However much the actors (including Robert Menzies, Geoffrey Rush, Gillian Jones and Kerry Walker) gained from participating in Lighthouse, it was a results-driven project, whose *raison d'être* was the cultivation of new Australian writing. Sharman may also have been looking to forge a legacy: a prototype state theatre ensemble which might influence the shape of similar projects in the future. Not surprising then that Nevin looked to it for inspiration, even though her chief interest was the cultivation of 'good acting'.

Two other Australian theatre ensembles deserving mention here share traits with both the guru and institutional prototypes. The short-lived Paris Theatre Company (1978), a breakaway from the Old Tote in its dying months, brought together the two directors of this time most committed to the possibilities of ensemble, Cramphorn and Sharman. Again, Robyn Nevin was among its actors. Perhaps the most likely reason (among many) for its premature collapse was the conflict of driving impulses between Cramphorn (mostly 'process') and Sharman (mainly 'results').

The 2005 opening season of Malthouse in Melbourne (previously the Playbox) is also of note.

This new company launched with an ensemble of actors working on two plays (Patrick White's *The Ham
Funeral* and Tom Wright's *Journal of the Plague Year*),
both directed by Michael Kantor. Two members of
the original Malthouse ensemble, Dan Spielman and
Marta Dusseldorp, went on to join the AC. While
Malthouse's debut season was well received, the
ideal of an in-house acting ensemble for Melbourne's
second-largest theatre company proved impossible to
sustain: it was both too expensive, and beyond the
company's available human resources.

There were lessons in all these projects for Robyn
Nevin, beacons of hope and warning lights. As she
said, 'Be careful what you pray for.'

Nevin's dream

Throughout her career, Nevin carried particularly fond memories of her 'prentice years' with
Rex Cramphorn's Performance Syndicate, when
she learnt about 'the gentleness, the courtesy and
the inclusiveness that is absolutely essential to any
rehearsal process and the importance of everybody
being in the room all the time and owning all of the
information equally'.

Nevin also looked back with high regard on
what her Old Tote experience had taught her about
acting craft and 'professional standards'. Most of her
subsequent career—as actor, director and ultimately
artistic director—was spent within this 'institutional',
state company model. But it was a system which, in
her view, had never adequately explored the innate
potential of actors. State theatres in Australia had

come to be little more than sausage-making factories. The challenge she set herself was to give good theatre-making, with fine acting at its core, a fresh chance—within the unwieldy structure of one of these large organizations. And in the creation of her ideal acting ensemble, Robyn Nevin envisioned a merging of the best of both systems that had shaped her.

Tom Wright, who had worked with both Australian Nouveau Theatre and Gilgul, joined Nevin as an artistic associate in December 2003. A *Sydney Morning Herald* interview makes clear that Wright knew at the time of his appointment of Robyn's dream: 'The long-term plan under the aegis of the NSW Government is to have a genuine ensemble of twelve fully paid professionals for twelve months at a time, an annual core company which will help to develop more audience loyalty' (2 December 2003). Wright, who was Nevin's close associate throughout the life of the AC, believes her vision was shaped less by commercial imperatives than by a knot of discontent over the way directors generally treated actors in Australia:

> Fundamentally, Robyn is an actor. She has an actor's dislike of being told what to do, whilst acknowledging its necessity. Much utopian dreaming about ensembles comes from actors who want more ownership of the process, as they feel continually shut out, always the bridesmaid to creativity.

But Nevin also knew that an ensemble operating within a large state company would need management, if not artistic direction. Could she possibly run both the ensemble *and* the main company? Part of her wanted to. Furthermore, she wanted to be an active participant in the project—in Wright's words, 'both an actor within the group and the boss'.

Nevin may have been driven by personal nostalgia for 'lost times', but that is not to detract from her high ambition to create the finest acting ensemble she could. But, in all practicality, were the two generic versions of an actors' ensemble compatible? While Nevin's heart may still have been with Cramphorn, her head had well and truly been shaped by the years she had spent as part of the institutional ensemble model. Was she struggling, subconsciously, to bring together two divided parts of her former self?

The question of leadership runs through the entire history of the AC, and it is important to record that Nevin searched extensively, within the limited time-frame permitted her, to find a suitable candidate—other than herself. While she admits that, as artistic director of the STC, she wanted to retain control over the key decisions shaping the ensemble's work, her preference was for someone else to lead the ensemble on the ground. Though names were put forward—Kosky, Benedict Andrews, Kosky & Andrews, Julian Meyrick—none was thought 'right'. This failure to find a 'first among equals'—should that read 'to decide between democracy and autocracy'?—was to underpin many of the conflicts that lay ahead. The person she did appoint as her close associate was Tom Wright, whom Nevin had met in 1998, when Kosky took his Bell Company *King Lear* to Brisbane: 'I wanted that brain', she says. Though Wright, running behind the scenes, was closer to the action than anyone else over the long term, he was never considered an AC member.

Choosing the ensemble

Why should the group be limited to twelve? Because that was as many as the budget could afford. It was an acceptable number for an organic 'self-selecting' tribe like Cramphorn's Performance Syndicate or the Keene/Taylor Theatre Project. But that is not to say that it would fit easily inside the vast machinery of a twenty-first-century state theatre company with a subscriber base and (necessarily) long lead times for marketing and venue allocation.

In selecting her twelve, Nevin asked several of her peers, including directors Kosky and Benedict Andrews, to suggest suitable actors. While Kosky says that he supported some of them, her final choices were dictated by Nevin's own instincts, not outsiders' suggestions.

At the top of her list were two of Australia's most capable senior men: John Gaden and Peter Carroll. Gaden says he turned down his original offer—to appear as a 'guest'—on the grounds that full-time members of the troupe would object to big names being parachuted in. He was right: the final twelve declared a suspicion of 'drop-ins' and endorsed Nevin's model of what we might call a 'Holy Twelve'. By that time Gaden had been offered a full-time placement. In fact, Gaden and Peter Carroll were both offered similar places, and both accepted.

The Melbourne meeting

Not long after the money came through, a meeting was held in Melbourne with potential candidates Pamela Rabe, Robert Menzies, Marco Chiappi, Eden Falk and Dan Spielman, at which Nevin, with Tom Wright beside her, tested the waters with her basic vision for the ensemble. It was a lengthy and passionate meeting and a good many questions were put to her. Not all of them were answered—at least, not to everyone's satisfaction.

Offers subsequently went out to those actors who attended. Menzies declined due to family commitments. Chiappi initially accepted, but had to withdraw when his father fell ill. Senior actress Pamela Rabe—with 'leadership qualities, a work ethic and director potential', said Nevin—accepted. She would more than fulfil Nevin's expectations.

Having already flagged an interest in working with the ensemble whatever its make-up, Kosky asked Nevin to consider Spielman, a young Melbourne actor who had made a name for himself in the Keene/Taylor Theatre Project even before he took part in the inaugural Malthouse season. Despite some doubts that arose at the Melbourne meeting—Dan kept asking, 'Why? But why do this?'—Nevin offered him a place. Spielman's worries never left him, however: he is what you call 'a thinking actor'. Nevin explained that it was not about 'going off into a desert with a guru'. Spielman knew full well what the model was; what he didn't know was how the ensemble might operate within the superstructure of a state theatre company. This was the challenge—one to which he was attracted, but also, he felt, one that needed extensive discussion. He was also interested in the project's intended legacy. As he puts it, while Nevin was looking back to Australian theatre culture's past, he was looking forward towards its future.

Nevin's ambition for the project, as she expounded it in Melbourne, was threefold: 'to distinguish the STC from other state companies'; 'to give actors an opportunity to develop their skills', and 'to give audiences a better experience'. 'These are my reasons', she said, 'and I think they are enough.' This was a laudable ambition, and likely to be fulfilled. But, apart from promising that under such circumstances the actors would 'just get better at their craft', Nevin threw no light on what they would actually do.

Dan Spielman was not alone in wanting more than that, but he went ahead and accepted the offer. After all, perhaps it was unreasonable to expect that all questions could be answered in advance. A certain amount of good faith and goodwill were required. And, initially, both of these were there in abundance. One only has to read the press articles that anticipated the company's first day in a rehearsal room to feel how palpable the excitement was.

More casting

After the Melbourne meeting, Nevin turned to completing the make-up of the Holy Twelve. Mid-career artist Brandon Burke was considered a valuable utility actor, able to fit in around other bigger names. Another experienced actor, Marta Dusseldorp, was seen to have a strong technique and had worked previously in ensembles, so she 'knew the world'. It was Deborah Mailman's 'bright shining quality', as much as her Aboriginality, that earned her an invitation. The strongly masculine Colin Moody was a late choice to replace Chiappi.

Four young actors, all of whose work Nevin had seen, were selected. An offer was made to Eden Falk after the Melbourne meeting. Martin Blum, Amber McMahon and Hayley McElhinney were selected after extensive auditions.

What shouts most loudly from this idiosyncratic line-up is the absence of a senior actress. Both Gaden and Carroll were already in their sixties, Rabe on the other hand was not yet 50 and Dusseldorp is younger than Rabe. To those who could read between the lines, the missing name was that of arguably Australia's finest female actor, Robyn Nevin herself. The ensemble was her baby and she wanted 'to be a force in the company'. According to Barrie Kosky—who thought two more senior women were needed, one about Rabe's age and another older—Nevin had originally planned to act in his production of *The Lost Echo*, but withdrew when she committed herself to directing Brecht's *Mother Courage*. Kosky was also indicating that two more men, masculine types in their mid-forties, would be useful.

Nevin acknowledges that she had originally hoped for an ensemble of thirteen members, with herself participating in at least some productions. After all, she was on salary and came at no extra cost. However, her commitments as the STC's artistic director meant she had no idea how much time she might have to devote to the ensemble. She could not simply come and go, that went against the core idea of the ensemble. Privately she would have liked the Board to let her step down from the artistic direction of the STC and devote herself fully to running the AC, but, as she said, 'The Board was not going to allow me to do that.'

On the subject of money, no parity pay structure was ever envisioned: the actors would be paid what each was worth. Ultimately, as the actors confirmed, there were five pay categories: the most senior members earned $100,000 a year; others had $75,000, and $60,000. The four least experienced were paid either $47,000 or just under $40,000 for no less work, but what might have been thought the chance of a life-time. In the AC's second season the two lowest categories were both raised a peg.

While early on Nevin talked about the ensemble working together for up to five years, the offer she finally made to each actor was specified as 'three years of close work'. Given the number of unknowns involved, she thought this a happy compromise, and it was one for which Bob Carr's money allowed. Nonetheless, most of the actors were disinclined to commit so far ahead. In the end, contracts were signed for an initial 18-month period, with an option for at least another year after that.

Once programming decisions had been made, work was scheduled to begin towards the middle of 2006.

2

The Rush to Succeed

Most directors cannot help actors [...].
That's why I wanted to be a force in the
company, so that I could guide, help the
acting standards. An impossible plan as it
turned out.

Robyn Nevin

The Cherry Orchard: a false dawn

In their first twelve months of operation, members
of the AC were given the opportunity to work
with four leading directors: Robyn Nevin, Barrie
Kosky, Jean-Pierre Mignon and Benedict Andrews, all
Australian, two resident and two visiting, each with a
different approach to making work.

Things might have begun very differently. In
December the previous year, 2005, the main STC
company had presented Chekhov's *The Cherry Orchard*
at Wharf One, with a cast that included future AC
members Peter Carroll, John Gaden, Pamela Rabe, Dan
Spielman and Robyn Nevin. The production was in
the hands of Howard Davies, considered by *Guardian*
critic Michael Billington to be 'Britain's best director'.

Nevin had a taste for the current British style of
theatre and for years had wanted Davies to work

with the STC. Indeed, she quietly hoped that his *Cherry Orchard* might have included more actors from the pending ensemble than was ultimately the case—indeed, that it might have been their inaugural production. If it was ever the case that Davies was offered the artistic directorship of the AC, he did not accept. Perhaps this was just as well: while several of the actors loved his approach, ironically the one least able to forge a happy bond with him was Nevin herself.

A starting plan

It is difficult to know how many ideas for start-up projects were considered before final decisions were made. One intriguing possibility was an experimental *King Lear*, developed over twelve weeks, initially for the STC Education Program, with up to three Lears, one to be played by a woman. How long this idea was entertained is hard to know, but its rejection was perhaps inevitable: 'Considering how much the AC was going to cost [in salaries]', said Wright, 'I think an education show with a rehearsal [period] that long would have been unbelievably indulgent.'

Finally, it was announced, at the 2006 season launch, that the ensemble would begin work in March of that year and face their first audience in May. Three productions were announced: a work based on Ovid and Euripides, entitled *The Lost Echo*, directed by Barrie Kosky; then Molière's *The Bourgeois Gentleman*, directed by Jean-Pierre Mignon. But it was in Brecht's *Mother Courage and her Children* that the Holy Twelve would first show their mettle.

Although it was essentially a catholic mix of classical work, on paper the ensemble's inaugural season looked promising. However, the AC actors themselves played no part in the programming, there had never been any question of the ensemble selecting their own repertoire. The season was to be composed exclusively of mainstream gigs. Yes, there would be voice lessons, and perhaps movement classes, but no alternative work of the kind conjured up by sitting cross-legged on bare boards in clouds of incense. And no alternative means of making work. While some were happy to do as they were told, others were required, as it were, to suspend their disbelief.

Mother Courage and her Children: a split in the family

Mother Courage was allocated a rehearsal period of seven weeks, less than the short-lived *King Lear* might have enjoyed, but markedly longer than most state theatre-company productions around Australia get. Pamela Rabe was cast as the eponymous heroine, a role which Nevin had considered taking on herself—until she conceded that it would be 'disruptive and wrong for the principle of ensemble', if she were to start by acting in the ensemble, only to be obliged later by her administrative responsibilities to pull out. She decided instead to direct the play—'because', she said, 'it was my ensemble, and I wanted to be […] across it all the way through.'

So there we have it: the term 'ensemble', meaning a coherent, finite number of individuals, was to cover the actors, and only the actors, and would exclude directors and other 'creatives'. Nevin's initial plan for herself was to be 'a guiding creative force': 'I wanted to guide the ensemble, be an influence on it. The strongest aspect of my directing is helping actors.' And it's true that, despite a major incident during rehearsals, by opening night, on 17 May 2006, everybody on stage looked good. Nevin had coaxed excellent performances out of each and every one of them.

Up and running

The story of the STC Actors Company is not all about Robyn Nevin, but she does tend to predominate in its first year. And while some may accuse this essay of being unduly critical of her personality, state of mind and way of going about things, it must be said that, in generously long interviews with the writer, her reflections on her own conduct in those early days have been no less critical. Furthermore, no matter how turbulent were the times that lay ahead, Nevin today remains hugely admired by almost all the original dozen for bringing the project into being, and standing by it, and each of them, through thick and thin.

The actors gathered on 20 March 2006 for their first day together. Predictably, they felt a heady mix of excitement and anticipation. They were a crack team, and they all knew that the eyes of many in the profession would be following their progress closely. A number of questions still hung in the air unanswered, however. Everyone knew, of course, what it said in the 2006 season brochure, but the actors had still not been gathered together as a group to discuss their aims and the way/s in which they might go about achieving them. Nevertheless, they arrived with open minds and in a spirit of goodwill.

In the event, what they got proved disappointing. It is true that attendance was very high—the entire company is usually invited to these events—and Nevin's welcoming remarks underlined the significance of the project. However, there was virtually no talk about dreams and ideals, and the focus quickly moved to *Mother Courage* and what needed to be done to get it up before an audience. Peter Carroll, for one, had hoped for an opportunity to be involved in discussions about production design, but, clearly, at least on this first production, there would be no inclusiveness of that kind. Actors were being squeezed into their predestined roles in the scheme of things. Cogs, yet again, in an all-too-familiar machine.

Day One of actual rehearsals and the actors were raring to go, but their director, as Nevin herself admits, was not. Not only had *The Cherry Orchard* been a trying, draining experience, but, in the meantime, she had also taken her production of Ibsen's *Hedda Gabler*, starring Cate Blanchett, to New York's Brooklyn Academy of Music. It had opened there on 2 March.

When she arrived to begin this important new project, Nevin was virtually just off the plane, and in a state of profound exhaustion. To some in the company she appeared uptight and defensive, and not particularly open to ideas from the floor. As anxieties escalated through the rehearsal period, one actor ultimately accused her of being 'poorly prepared'. They were working on one of the major works of the modern classical repertoire and some of them wanted time to be set aside to discuss the ensemble's *raison d'être* and long-term goals, and what part Brecht played in these.

While Nevin remembered with enormous admiration Rex Cramphorn's rehearsal process, she drew on only parts of his approach. She certainly expected all the actors to be in the room all the time, but the creative environment she fostered was not nearly as soft or imaginatively spacious as her predecessor's is remembered to have been. 'Gentleness, courtesy and inclusiveness' are not the first words most actors would use when describing Nevin's directorial method.

Nor was it productive. Time in the rehearsal room was not spent observing fellow actors grow in their roles. Instead, hours were taken up looking on while issues relating to Mother Courage's cart, and how it might be dragged around the stage, were resolved, and working through what came to be called the 'transitions', choreographed business linking Brecht's scenes. The actors not directly involved in these activities became increasingly frustrated. There were no complaints, but, as one actor recalls, 'It was unbearable being in the room sometimes and it was clear not everyone was happy.'

In Nevin's view, chatting at length about direction and goals was a waste of time. A group of actors did not by definition constitute an ensemble. And no amount of talk could create one. An ensemble, she believed, came into being *after and as a result of* working together on one play after another. As far as she was concerned, they were on track. In retrospect, Nevin accepts that she misread the signs and that two conflicting agendas were running concurrently.

There were exciting moments too, of course, during the *Mother Courage* rehearsals. Spielman remembers the day Colin Moody stepped beyond the general tentativeness in the room and delivered a fearless, bellowing version of 'The Cook's Song'. In doing so, he was the first to break the ice, and everyone in the room was thrilled. This is worth remembering, because it demonstrates Moody's enthusiasm, at least in the early days, to give fully to the project.

After a month of 'non-discussion', the actors took matters into their own hands and, during a lunchtime break, organized their own meeting. It was Easter Monday, 17 April 2006. As the day was a public holiday, the Wharf was almost empty, so they met on one of the outside verandahs. When Nevin, who had returned to her office to attend to other STC matters, became aware of the gathering, she went out to ask what was going on. They were merely 'throwing a few ideas around', they said. Nevin wanted to know why she had not been invited. It was 'an actors' meeting', they replied, to which Nevin exclaimed, 'But I am an actor too!' The meeting broke up in befuddled bemusement.

While no offence had been intended, with hindsight, several actors agree that not informing Nevin of the meeting might have been a mistake. But they looked forward to what usually happens after similar lovers' quarrels, kissing and making up. Not on this occasion, however. When rehearsal resumed not long afterwards, Nevin threw her head back with stoic resolution and declared that, despite the grievous blow to her status, there was nothing to be done but carry on. Peter Carroll was unable to let the matter rest: he even admits to having raised his voice. Some of the newcomers became quite fearful. Looking back, Tom Wright believes he made a critical error. He had been employed to work for and with Nevin, and should have stayed at her side. Instead, he moved to another part of the room, detaching himself and leaving her further isolated.

While *Mother Courage* went ahead and played to good notices, there is no avoiding the brutal fact that something terrible had happened that Easter Monday. It was not immediately apparent, but a wedge had been driven between Nevin and the actors. After so much work in getting the ensemble started, Nevin could not get over the feeling that she had been profoundly betrayed. It seemed to her that she had given birth to a spider that ate its own mother.

3

Directorial Style: Three Different Australians

Some need carrot, others need stick.

Barrie Kosky

After the experience of *Mother Courage*, Robyn Nevin finally decided that it was impossible for her to play anything more than a supervisory role with the Actors Company: no acting and no more directing. But, the emotional breach between herself and the Holy Twelve now becoming a physical one, even running the project from her office was likely to prove testing. No-one else had ever been appointed to lead the ensemble artistically and, as the STC's artistic director, she had many other responsibilities. Moreover, while her removal from further active artistic engagement with the ensemble might have brought clarity to an ambiguous situation, it also burnt an important bridge. As Nevin stepped back from the front line, her shadow, Tom Wright, also felt obliged to remove himself. To replace him, Stage Manager Malcolm Hughes was upgraded to AC Company Manager; and then, when he left at the end of 2006, Egil Kipste took on this role in 2007. For the final year, the job fell to Millie Mullinar. But all were little more than 'runners', taking messages from the ensemble's camp to that of STC management, which for all practical purposes was Nevin herself.

Spielman thought that Nevin's withdrawal left a 'vacuum of leadership that had a huge number of knock-on effects'. Not everyone sees it that way: Gaden, for example, acknowledges the wounding, but says that by the time the ensemble's second production was under way Nevin, ever the professional, had bounced back. Kipste agrees.

'Robyn was one-hundred per cent interested in what was happening and would have regular meetings at the beginnings and ends of projects—and other times, if an issue came up. Sometimes Rob Brookman would come in on it as well.' She would monitor the progress of a guest director through the rehearsal phase, sit in on dress rehearsals and offer feedback, drop into dressing rooms before opening night; and her office door was always open to the actors. Indeed, in an effort to keep up with their progress and concerns, she spent many hours with them in one-to-one meetings.

That may well be true, but the fact remains that, while 'management' may have been in place, artistic leadership had disappeared from the heart of the AC after *Mother Courage*, and had never been replaced.

The Lost Echo:
the ensemble finds its way

For the moment, problems to do with leadership were swept away, as attention was turned towards the new director, the charismatically controversial Barrie Kosky. He had arrived from his new home in Vienna midway through the seven-week season of *Mother Courage*. Having been given the brief of taking the company on as exciting an adventure as he could concoct, he created *The Lost Echo*, which ran for more than seven hours and included not only a guest appearance by cabaret artist Paul Capsis as the goddess Diana (a pig-tailed schoolgirl spluttering venom in classical Greek), but also the participation of 22 second-year students from NIDA. Already the Troy-like walls put up to protect the 'unity of the ensemble' had been breached—but to good artistic effect.

Kosky worked with a text reconfigured by Tom Wright from writings by Ovid and Euripides; and, in the last of four parts, the lyrics of Schubert's *Die Winterreise*. He got on very well with Nevin, who admired him for the high status he gave to actors and acting: 'He is the great director. He and Rex are the only two who have done it for me,' she says. One big difference between Kosky and Cramphorn, however, is that Kosky leads from the front. He is hugely demanding in the rehearsal room, but at the end of the day there will be hugs all round.

Aware that there had been problems during *Mother Courage*, Kosky made it clear that he wanted a fresh start, with a change of pace and tone. Four weeks of morning rehearsals were arranged during the second half of the *Mother Courage* run, and they focused on tango-dancing and singing lessons. Physically demanding, but more fun than even a happy Brecht production. In the seven further weeks of full-time rehearsal after *Mother Courage* ended, days were divided up into three and different aspects of the production worked on concurrently. If the actors worked hard, Kosky worked harder—ten- to twelve-hour days—as he moved from taking individual actors through long monologues from Ovid, setting a new reading of *The Bacchae* in a filthy toilet block, choreographing swirling bar scenes with the NIDA students, to working closely with Peter Carroll, who was required, in Part Four, to sing almost the entire *Die Winterreise* cycle, with his 34 fellow cast members in support.

It is hard to exaggerate the dimensions of the *Lost Echo* project. The work was created virtually from scratch, and ensemble members were offered intense participation in its creation. Kosky approached it as a field commander might a military attack. Fall-back positions and improvised sorties were *de rigueur*. Where no suitable actor was available, Kosky and Wright cut swathes through their text, and individuals—snipers, ambulance officers, kamikaze pilots—were cultivated to work to their strengths. Remarkable things happened. Just one example: when Kosky asked young Amber McMahon to try singing a song another way, a fantastic blues voice emerged that she never knew she had. By now the younger actors were learning from observing the seniors at work, just as Nevin had hoped. This pedagogical bond evolved steadily over the next year and beyond.

Not every one of the actors enjoyed working with Kosky. Some found him too invasive. But he has enormous authority as well as deftness in the rehearsal room and, massive as the schedule was, he worked with each individual in a different way to draw out the best from them: 'Some need carrot, others need stick.' When Colin Moody spat the dummy, in a scene that unnerved the others, Kosky closed the incident down promptly and positively, cleverly and without stick. When Moody asked if he could wear a leather jockstrap through the final act, with helium-filled balloons tied to his nipple rings, Kosky said 'Yes'.

I mention this now because, with Spielman, Moody emerged as the other major malcontent, and other directors found him difficult to handle. Also a 'thinking' actor, Moody is more volatile than Spielman. His complaints about 'approach'—he had run-ins with almost every director—may well have been legitimate; but his argument was often lost in the startling manner in which he expressed himself on these occasions.

The end result was astonishing. While some who saw it thought it a curate's egg, there can be little argument that in *The Lost Echo*, between them, Kosky and the AC created one of the most dazzlingly original works seen on the Sydney stage for some considerable time. For the actors it was a dream come true: they were finally on song, each of them pushed to their limits both in rehearsal and also in what they were finally called on to do onstage.

The success of *The Lost Echo*—and the present writer is not alone in considering it a brilliant achievement—is in large measure attributable to Robyn Nevin, who had fought so tenaciously to establish an AC in the first place and to bring in someone like Kosky to push so many of the company to unsuspected limits. Nevin may well be noted for her mercurial moods, but she is also the great encourager. And few in Australia had given Kosky the kind of unflinching support that allowed a monumental enterprise like *The Lost Echo* to be created and to succeed so spectacularly.

The Bourgeois Gentleman:
he trips on the stairs

The first thing you noticed on entering the Sydney Theatre's large auditorium to see the AC's next production, Molière's 1670 *comédie-ballet*, *The Bourgeois Gentleman*, was the set. While *The Lost Echo* had been huge in concept, and on the same stage, much of the space was left bare, allowing the actors' imaginations to freely take flight. Here was a monument of contemporary stagecraft in which the salient feature was a massive staircase that ran from the top of the proscenium stage-left down to the stage floor—and then further down, into the bowels of the building. Perhaps it had been conceived as a symbol of the *bourgeois* Monsieur Jourdain's pointless attempts to climb the social ladder. (You have to be born a *gentilhomme*!) Unfortunately, that appears not to have been the case. It existed primarily so that extravagantly costumed actors might make their entrance, skittle down at comically high speed and disappear into the substage darkness. In short, the production proved merely a colourful period farce with little to say about class, or about the class distinctions that lie at the heart of the play. This was surprising. After all, although much of director Jean-Pierre Mignon's most recent work had been in television and opera, his invitation to participate in the AC's first season was presumably based on his reputation as a director of Molière in the 1980s and '90s with his Australian Nouveau Theatre, in Melbourne. He had also directed a quite successful STC production of *The Miser* in 2004, starring John Gaden.

Kosky in the rehearsal room would have been a hard act for anybody to follow, especially since the actors' schedule had allocated them no rest or breathing-space: as Spielman puts it, 'No time to grieve'. This became a pattern. While Brookman and his financial team had factored in productions at the new Sydney Theatre, they had underestimated their costs, and this put enormous pressure on scheduling. There was no time for niceties or side-projects, such as readings, yoga classes etc. All extras fell away, as guest directors fought for every unfilled hour to get their show up and looking good.

The Bourgeois Gentleman was the AC's third show and, six months into the project, the actors were still being denied any meaningful input into the way the production was to be conceived or designed. What kind of an ensemble was this again? The massive machinery that ran the rest of the STC had assumed the upper hand. In the title role of Monsieur Jourdain, Peter Carroll was presented with a translation he found difficult to bring to life, but was denied permission to stray from it. The company as a whole found Mignon's laid-back approach to rehearsing frustrating after the great riff they had just enjoyed with Kosky. While the comfortable, unchallenging production that emerged did little to please those of us who prefer our theatre bold, it was very much to the taste of STC subscribers—and many of them wrote in to say so. While

Carroll still looks back on the production with little enthusiasm, Spielman, at the time underwhelmed, now acknowledges that in the role of the Ballet Master he was stretched as an actor to an extent he did not then appreciate.

The Bourgeois Gentleman exposed two problems that would haunt the rest of the company's life. First, when directors like Mignon found themselves faced with a 'classic', which by temperament they were disinclined to 'creatively rearrange' (as Kosky or Andrews might), the fixed number and gender of ensemble players at their disposal constituted a major constraint. Mignon had no choice but to work with the actors he had been given—and match them to the roles as best he could.

Second, as Pamela Rabe observed, when an actor is offered a role, it is accompanied by a tacit, unwritten contract. As rehearsals unfold, for better or worse, the actor accepts that they have agreed to co-operate fully with the director. This was not the case with the AC: to the very end, directors and texts were foisted on the ensemble by management, sometimes with no discussion. This was to prove increasingly problematic in the second year, as certain actors and particular guest directors failed to bond naturally.

It seems astonishing now, but *The Bourgeois Gentleman*—only the third ensemble production—was in fact the last time the original twelve appeared together as the AC. Natural causes initially took a hand. By the end of 2006, Marta Dusseldorp and Deborah Mailman were both pregnant and, as a result, were absent for the entire 2007 season.

The actors had been given the opportunity to comment on certain options for the 2007 program, which had been announced in late September. *Troupers*, a play by Michael Cove, was rejected and relocated in the STC's mainstream program. And other possibilities, including a new script by Louis Nowra, also failed to win approval. But, in the end, with time breathing down her neck, Nevin made the final decisions (as was her wont anyway): four mainstage works, each to involve the full ensemble. Patrick White's *The Season at Sarsaparilla*, to be directed by arguably Australia's brightest young director, Benedict Andrews; *The Art of War*, a new play written for them by British dramatist Stephen Jeffreys, to be directed by another Briton, Annabel Arden; *A Midsummer Night's Dream*, to be directed by an emerging British director, Ed Dick; and *Tales from Vienna Woods*, to be directed by Jean-Pierre Mignon.

The year 2006 and the AC's first season drew to a close on a lower note than the name Molière might usually imply. But, squeezed in before Christmas, was a week's—'physical, but not too intense, and quite refreshing'—workshop on *A Midsummer Night's Dream*. 'It made us look forward to what we were going to do with [this play]', recalls Eden Falk, who also has memories of Dan Spielman and himself grabbing brooms and sweeping out the AC's main rehearsal room. After quite a tough year this felt cathartic, a cleansing and a purging—and not just physically. Then it was off to the STC Christmas party and, for the entire ensemble, a well-earned four-week break.

The Season at Sarsaparilla:
a masterpiece

The obligation to cast a play with a finite number of actors can occasionally produce unexpectedly success-ful results. Who would have guessed that the casting of Peter Carroll as lemon-lipped tots-mom (aka mother of two fine girls), Girlie Pogson, in Patrick White's *The Season at Sarsaparilla* would produce such a highlight of the AC's three seasons and one of Carroll's finest portrayals in a long and celebrated career. He was not alone: in Andrews' radical rendition of this Australian 'classic', every member of the ensemble was given a chance and grabbed it with both hands. *Sarsaparilla* would take its place beside *The Lost Echo*, a palpable hit and an absolute chart-buster!

The second season started in high spirits, on Monday, 15 January 2007. There is something marvelous about working at the Wharf at this time of year, with the Harbour at its most majestic. The bright sun and burning heat of those summer days seemed to assist the actors in bringing to fresh life White's extraordinary text about ordinary suburban Australians, a play in which the midsummer weather is almost a character in itself.

Again the concept and design were presented to the actors as *faits accomplis*, and a few were wary of Andrews' reputation as an auteur. But reservations quickly fell away when they discovered what the direc-tor and his set designer Robert Cousins had in mind. White's three identikit 1950s suburban Australian homes were to be folded into one. The three families that constitute the core characters would all be living under one roof—under *Big Brother*-like video surveillance. When Pamela Rabe as Nola Boyle, the sultry bitch on heat, went to put on her lipstick, she would stare not into a mirror, but the lens of a video camera. A tiny action like this is not easy to execute, especially when on each side of the proscenium large screens would be magnifying the action. One tiny smudge would shatter the conceit that what we were seeing was 'real life'.

From the very first day of rehearsals, the actors worked on a fully realized set, built in that main rehearsal room—the tiled roof, louvred windows, every stick of furniture, and the cameras, all in place. On stage the house would revolve: in rehearsals, as they moved from one scene to the next, desks and chairs were picked up and repositioned as the director and his crew simply 'revolved' themselves.

Benedict Andrews' reputation as a control freak has less to do with inhibiting the creativity of his actors than with a need for precision in the high formality of his stagings. Intense directorial intervention was exactly what this production required. Yet, within the complexities of how not to get in each other's way, every actor found their way to an extraordinary personal truth and power.

Both individually and as one, the ensemble produced stunning work. While Andrews believes he could have created this work with actors specially chosen, he is quick to confess that in the AC he found a deftness and rapport, a mutual trust and knowingness, that allowed them to work very quickly. Although they were not yet one calendar year into their life together, and in only their fourth production, individual actors felt it safe to take risks. They would try things they would never have dared try in a one-off production. And fellow actors felt free to comment, offer feed-back—on the floor or, more discreetly, after rehearsal.

A further point should be made about this beauti-ful production. Directed by John Tasker, the play was premiered in Adelaide in 1962. Even after Jim Sharman's popular 1976 revival, doubts continued to be entertained about its 'authenticity' as a dramatic text. To many it was still an idiosyncratic foible created 'on the side' by a gifted novelist. Benedict Andrews' AC production swept all misgivings away: it can now stand for what it really is, one of Australia's greatest works for the theatre.

If ever there was an Australian production that deserved to seen by the rest of the world, it was this one. For me, in my 30 years of following and writing about the making of Australian theatre, this produc-tion represents, both culturally and creatively, the highest point. An onstage Everest. This production alone makes me grateful that the AC— however pain-ful its birth-pangs, and regardless of the tantrums and tears along the way—was brought into existence.

4

The Concept Hits the Fan

You could not ask this question 'Why are
we doing this work?' in a rehearsal room
at the STC.

Dan Spielman

I n the course of the second year, as novelty and
surprise gave way to routine, problems arising from
the absence of an artistic director began to show like
cracks in a wall. Nevin stuck to her plan of throwing
fresh experiences at the ensemble in the form of one-
off guest directors. But without a more explicit *raison
d'être* or a clearly articulated way of going about things,
the proposition that this was a project that privileged
the actor began to look frail.

Other systemic problems concerning the
'administration' of the project were also beginning
to show. The workload was enormous, but still
more debilitating was the lack of breaks between
productions, which meant that, as work on one
show overlapped with work on another, there was
no 'thinking time' for consolidation and renewal.
Rehearsing by day and performing at night might
be the model for the big European companies, but
those are huge ensembles that work in repertoire,

with actors alternating leading roles with bit-parts and resources provided for extended time out.

Still, twelve months had passed, and no time had been set aside to ask whether a clear sense of purpose was beginning to emerge out of the work. It is not surprising, therefore, that, in the absence of artistic leadership, the ensemble began to accumulate its own power and took to solving matters themselves—at least those over which they had some control, which unfortunately did not include relations with the STC at large. The actors talked among themselves, incessantly and in a spirit of enormous goodwill. All of them desperately wanted the project—not just the next production—to be successful.

To the credit of its members, an incredibly sturdy culture of mutual support had already evolved. Dusseldorp says that she looked out for Carroll during his difficult time with the Molière; in turn the seniors, Carroll and Gaden, offered inspiration, support and guidance to the younger members; and Rabe emerged as the nurturing 'wolf mother' the ensemble sorely lacked. The camaraderie was potent to the point of intimidating outsiders—the kind of intensity that is formed, suggested one actor, when 'you are confronted by a common enemy'.

While Nevin stayed as close to the project as she could from her office, nevertheless, a sense of 'them and us' began to colour relations. Frustration and distrust escalated as it was increasingly felt that the STC as a whole was not responding adequately to the ensemble's concerns. Administration might have found the AC increasingly pushy and demanding, but it had failed to establish a coherent framework within which ensemble members could work. For whatever reason, the lines of communication were simply not as open and flowing as they needed to be. Sadly, it was this that triggered the descent into the maelstrom that occurred over the course of the next two productions and left the Holy Twelve permanently damaged.

The Art of War:
conflict behind the scenes

Visiting director Annabel Arden had co-founded Theatre de Complicite with Simon McBurney, a UK ensemble renowned for its highly evolved 'actor-focused' process. *The Art of War* had been commissioned for the AC from playwright Stephen Jeffreys, who was Arden's husband. They had a proven track record as a husband-and-wife working partnership and certainly, from the stalls, *The Art of War* looked pretty good. No clues here that for some members of the AC the experience had been less than happy.

Unable to meet any of them or watch their work, Jeffreys had used photos of the actors as the basis of his characterisations. For some this was odd: 'So this is what he thinks of me?' was a common reaction to reading the script for the first time. And Arden arrived on the first day of rehearsal, having seen no more of the actors than a single performance of *Sarsaparilla* revealed.

The first problem was fatigue. The AC was yet again rehearsing a new play in the afternoon while performing at night. The Complicite method is very physical, 'creating things from the body,' says Hayley McElhinney, 'and we were very tired. […] It was like we were doing classes [and] it wasn't really suited to what we had become.' The delight of a second season of *Sarsaparilla*—'every night was exciting'—was being sapped by yet another, different approach to making work. 'We were constantly working with directors who did not know what we had done,' says McElhinney, 'We were having to rewrite the book each time.'

However good Arden might have been, to the actors she was a 'drop in'. Her process, however interesting, was not at all like the one which the ensemble by now was evolving for itself.

Of all the AC members, McElhinney is probably the most intuitive and open-hearted: Kosky described her as 'all nerve-endings'. There had been unhappiness during *Mother Courage*, but back then, she says, there was also still hope. Deep into rehearsals proper for *The Art of War*, even she was starting to lose heart: 'I walk into a room and I know how everyone feels. This time it was more of a malaise. […] It made me really sad for the first time.'

A Midsummer Night's Dream: what a nightmare

With Ed Dick's production of *A Midsummer Night's Dream* these concerns spiralled into a crisis. Arden may not have been in McBurney's league, but she was an experienced director who stuck to her guns—and, as far as audiences were concerned, she produced a good result. Dick was the youthful protégé of a different leading British director, Cheek by Jowl's Declan Donnellan, who had brought an excellent production of *Othello* to Australia in 2004. The week of fun spent on the text at Christmas 2006 had given the actors high hopes, but, as more weeks went by, rehearsals for *The Dream* sank them into a mire of despondency.

As Benedict Andrews has observed, the AC did its best work under strong leadership; and Dick was simply too inexperienced to withstand the combined forces of the increasingly self-empowered ensemble. At some point again during rehearsals for *The Art of War*, when he found Arden's sense of purpose too vague, Colin Moody had given vent to his feelings. But that was nothing compared to what occurred during *The Dream*: one day Moody brought rehearsal to a standstill with an outburst of fury that sent Ed Dick fleeing to Nevin, to the headmistress's office.

However much they might have sympathised with what were in fact common concerns, none of the group liked *the way* Moody would express himself. Worryingly, his outbursts were usually preceded by days of sulking, simply shutting down and refusing to engage openly in the rehearsal process. This was difficult for everyone, but, for those working in specific scenes with him, it was intolerable.

Senior Stage Manager Georgia Gilbert became familiar with the pattern and took to warning guest directors in advance whenever the volcano in Moody began to gurgle. Sometimes she would interrupt a rehearsal and call for a ten-minute break. This might confuse a director, but Gilbert kept her eye on Moody as tension built, usually around the time of the tech run, a few days before opening night. Unfortunately, there were times when even she was unable to predict an eruption.

Meanwhile, visiting directors were being offered their chance of a lifetime: extended rehearsal time, harbour views, and an open door to the STC's impressive technical / production resources. How could they resist putting their own interests before those of the ensemble, of whose deeper needs they had no inkling? Around this point, it has been suggested, 'The Actors Company' might have been better named 'A Directors' and Designers' Company'.

On the core question, 'Whose ensemble is this?', Moody was not the only actor to feel that, whenever differences arose, the STC administration sided with guest directors. 'Are we guns for hire,' asked Dusseldorp, 'or is someone choosing to work with us and come into our process? We talked about this a lot. Then we were told: "You cannot demand from a director that they come to your party." And we said: "But it *is* our party".'

As it turned out, it was not their party. This was confirmed when Moody was required to apologize to Ed Dick, and put on notice. Meaning, one more outburst and he was out—in response to which Moody drafted a letter of resignation. No wonder the production of Shakespeare's faerie-winged comedy seemed devoid of lightness and humour on opening night—indeed, for the entire run. In all but physical presence Moody had left. Others struggled. It was an even blacker reading than Dick's intentionally dark conception of the play.

Another problem faced by the actors when working with what would now become a succession of guest directors was that, in privileging their own reputations, the visitors tended to look to what each actor already did best. Young or old, actors were being asked to trot out the same familiar performance. What had this to offer them in the way of development? And particular actors were also partnered together time and time again. Pamela Rabe and Colin Moody had been a unit in *The Season at Sarsaparilla, The Art of War*, and now were paired for a third time in *The Dream*. This might not have happened, had Marta Dusseldorp returned on time from maternity leave. Ed Dick had wanted her to play Titania to Moody's Bottom, and in her absence Rabe was cast in her place. 'I'd done the play twice before and didn't understand the [idea of] this production at all,' says Dusseldorp. 'And I didn't see how it was going to interest audiences, unless [Dick] was going to have a full-on take with it, which he didn't. We had deduced that from the workshop.' Deborah Mailman declined to return at this point also.

It would appear to be that, however bright Ed Dick's prospects may be, at this early point in his career he was unable to meet the potential in the room. Pent up with frustration going back months now, Moody isolated his prey and ran him down.

Dan Spielman's story

It will be recalled that, from the time of that first meeting in Melbourne, Spielman—who had brought with him several years of experience with the Keene/ Taylor Theatre Project and had been a happy and productive member of an ensemble in the past—was anxious about 'purpose' and 'meaning'. And that he had been prepared to put aside preliminary doubts in the expectation that his concerns would be addressed once the project got under way. However, in his view, that never happened. Nevertheless, he remained a staunchly loyal and productive member of the team, and he turned in some remarkable performances, particularly in *The Lost Echo* and *Sarsaparilla*.

Courage comes easily to Spielman, and when Moody lost his temper and he saw fear in some of the actors' eyes, he stepped in and made himself a human shield. 'There are difficult people in the theatre,' he concedes. 'What we are trying to do is difficult. Of any workplace the theatre is one where [it] is not only tolerated […], but also very important—on a human level—to acknowledge people's rough edges.' Many of the best actors have a reputation for being extraordinarily 'difficult'. Not by choice, but by cast of fate or accident of birth, they have an inner vulnerability that predicates their rare capacity to inhabit other souls. It is the way in which these artists are treated that counts.

By the time *A Midsummer Night's Dream* was up and running, Spielman and Moody were sharing a dressing room and had become close confidants. Spielman, who wonders in hindsight if there wasn't an element of self-sabotage in his preparedness to soak up Moody's bile, was himself growing increasingly dissatisfied with the 'role of management' or lack thereof. Then his own engagement with *The Dream* hit a reef. It was decided late in rehearsals that, as Puck, he would 'fly', in other words, be harnessed up and, by means of ropes, work in the air. Neither Ed Dick nor Jane Gibson, the movement director Dick had brought with him from England, had any experience in this form of work. Spielman's first experience in the harness was at the tech run, one day before the show faced its first audience. Perhaps tiredness and a certain alienation contributed, but over the course of the season what he first felt as discomfort, then pain, evolved into a serious injury.

Perversely, the AC's regular movement director, Gavin Robins, who had a strong background in physical theatre and 'flying', had been banished from the rehearsal room to make way for the director's own movement specialist. When Robins' help was needed, he was nowhere to be found. For the next six months, Spielman had to undergo regular treatment.

Colin Moody announced his resignation to the ensemble well before *A Midsummer Night's Dream* closed. He would see out the season—a cheery prospect for those working with him on stage—but he was withdrawing forthwith from all other AC activities. It is not difficult to imagine the mood of the room. Understandably, Spielman was himself now near breaking-point. The company was on the verge of its second summer break, but he needed more than time off. He needed the STC to manifest some goodwill and good faith. With his agent by his side in the room, Spielman asked not to be cast in the next production.

It was a test as much as anything. The STC did not know it was being given a chance to redeem itself, as Spielman kept his cards close to his chest. If his request was not acceded to, he would resign: 'To me it [was] abundantly obvious why I should be given a break. I was a wreck. If there was not the [...] compassion in the company to make that possible without hesitation, if there was any attempt to negotiate, I was gone.'

The STC—the same company that had earlier granted two AC actresses twelve months' maternity leave—listened sympathetically, but ultimately refused his request, for fear of 'setting a precedent'. They asked later what would have happened if they had granted the request, but it was too late. Far too late. Spielman now believes that his departure, and Moody's, was necessary in order for the AC to continue to work and grow. He still hoped the ensemble would find its form, and he certainly never regarded his departure as 'proof of the project's failure'. Rather, he felt, it had been a case of 'this particular ensemble model [...] not [being able to] tolerate internal irritants'. Had the ensemble's embracing philosophy ever been clarified, as he had wished from the start, he might well have been able to adjust his ways to fit. It was 'devastating [that] we lost him,' says one AC member. Many others hold the same view.

We cannot speak for Colin Moody, except to say that his problems with the AC have not stood in the way of Benedict Andrews continuing to offer him work. While Spielman was gone, never to return, Moody did come back, at the beginning of 2008, to play in the Melbourne season of *The Season at Sarsaparilla*.

5

Zeitgeist:
The War Plays

> It was an extraordinary time [...] with that
> group of people.
>
> Cate Blanchett

There was a much-needed two-week break after the close of *A Midsummer Night's Dream*. Not only were the actors exhausted and dispirited, but casting adjustments were required for the next show, Odön von Horváth's 1931 *Tales from the Vienna Woods*, which was to be directed by Jean-Pierre Mignon. For those who might have wondered why Mignon, whose *Bourgeois Gentleman* had not been an entirely successful experience for either the actors or their audiences, the answer is that he had been booked for a second production well before the Molière had opened.

Tales from the Vienna Woods:
lost in translation

This unusual work, a 'take' on the traditional German folk play, that tells of daily life in contemporary Vienna. The STC program describes it as a 'satirical attack' on 'the complacency of townsfolk amidst the insidious rise of fascism'. While this was not a theme that crossed my mind as I watched it, perhaps the failure of this production—the actors seemed under-energised and the design excessive—cannot be laid entirely at Mignon's feet: he was returning to a company at its lowest emotional point. The Moody-Spielman ulcer had been lanced, and Steve Le Marquand and Luke Mullins, less problematic replacements, were helping heal the wound. Nonetheless, a number of those who had worked with Mignon before were nervous.

There were other changes. Sadly, Peter Carroll had recently been diagnosed with a serious illness and was obliged to take time out, but his shoes were ably filled by the younger, but no less authoritative, Robert Menzies. Meanwhile, the new mothers, Deborah Mailman and Marta Dusseldorp had returned. So did Paul Capsis, who dropped in, bringing some of his special magic to the role of the MC.

At the close of *Vienna Woods* (in mid-December 2007), the initial two-season contracts were due for renewal. The only actors who declined this opportunity were the self-effacing Martin Blum, who preferred to go off and see more of the world, and Deborah Mailman, who, after being back for just one play, decided to devote her energies to full-time motherhood. One suspects that, had either of them found life at the AC more rewarding, they might have chosen to stay. In seven plays so far, Blum, for example, had been given little opportunity to shine.

Given the unhappiness that many had supposedly endured, management anticipated that rather more of the original ensemble might have opted to leave. But they did not, and certainly no pressure was applied to anyone to go. It remains a question to this day why the STC clung to the vestiges of its original policy of a Holy Twelve. After all, it was already in tatters.

In the way the AC was set up, inadequate attention had been paid to where it might sit within the STC as a whole. If anything, it operated as a discrete unit, and in tough times, it seemed, in isolation. Tom Wright continues to believe that the *need* for an ensemble was never adequately argued to the company. To some full-time administrative staff, the AC was 'elitist, exclusive and invisible'. They were able to access their specially designated rehearsal rooms by the western walkway—which meant that some staff members never had a conversation with a single AC member during the entire time they shared the same building. Apart from Peter Carroll, who made it his business to walk through STC administration on many a morning say 'hello'. Yet let's imagine someone in the Accounts department, suggests Tom Wright: '"I don't understand," they might say. "You never see them and they get paid this absurd amount of money, [play in] absurdly expensive productions that don't do well financially and that I don't like."' This would hardly have been the fault of the AC members, but some of the staff might have felt that it was. Anyone with access to the figures would have known that, after the artistic director and the general manager, no one at the STC was more highly paid than senior members of the AC.

Then there were questions asked by the actors, by Marta Dusseldorp, for example. Why was there so little marketing or promotion of the AC? Why were the actors' names not splashed across the sides of Sydney buses? Why, in over three years, was Dusseldorp only asked to do one press interview? Some subscribers couldn't understand why they kept seeing the same faces on stage. And as for the plays' content! Was it the *Zeitgeist*, something in the post-9/11 air? Had the military conflict in Iraq, Afghanistan and 'troubles' in Palestine unwittingly cast their gloom over the AC's program? How many shows could the STC do on the subject of war and still maintain subscriber interest? In the AC's third year, just when subscriber alienation was becoming apparent in the figures, all three major productions were devoted to this same cheerless theme.

2008: Blanchett and Upton
take the reins

The AC took holidays for the last two weeks of 2007, after which a core group returned for a week's re-rehearsal, prior to a special Melbourne season of *The Season at Sarsaparilla*. Fortunately, Peter Carroll had re-covered sufficiently to reprise his extraordinary Girlie Pogson—to the consternation of some of Melbourne's matrons. As the curtain fell on a matinee that I at-tended there, a vigorous debate broke out among a group in my row over whether Girlie had been played by a man or a woman!

Meanwhile, back in Sydney, a number of impor-tant changes had taken place behind the scenes. As far back as *The Bourgeois Gentleman*, twelve months earlier, it had been announced that Robyn Nevin would be leaving the STC at the end of 2007, to be replaced by actor-and-writer, husband-and-wife team, Cate Blanchett and Andrew Upton. Given the required lead times, Nevin needed to schedule the 2008 season in advance of the new team's arrival, which meant that Blanchett and Upton had no creative input into the AC's program for the first year of their tenure. As it transpired, this caretaker season would include, after *Sarsaparilla* in Melbourne, *The Serpent's Teeth* (a Daniel Keene double-bill of *Citizens* and *Soldiers*); *Gallipoli*, a large-scale, group-devised work to be directed by Nigel Jamieson; and *The War of the Roses*, an eight-hour two-play reworking of Shakespeare's epic eight-play cycle of English history plays, by Tom Wright and Benedict Andrews. After a twelve-week rehearsal period, *The War of the Roses* was scheduled to open in January 2009, as part of that year's Sydney Festival.

Whatever their private thoughts regarding the AC and that year's programming, Upton and Blanchett could only sit back and watch—until Andrews invited Blanchett to join the AC for *The War of the Roses* in order to play the roles of Richard II and Lady Anne (in *Richard III*). She readily agreed.

The Serpent's Teeth: back with bite

For the members of the AC, Daniel Keene's contemporary anti-war double-bill is one of their most fondly remembered projects. They were now a happier unit, and the requirement that they should rehearse one new production while performing in another had been dropped. Best of all, at Robyn Nevin's suggestion, one of their own, Pamela Rabe, was to make her directorial debut. She directed the first play, *Citizens*, set in somewhere not unlike the Gaza Strip; and Tim Maddock, who had directed in Adelaide and Melbourne, taught at the University of Wollongong and was familiar with Keene's work, was in charge of the second, *Soldiers*. This play, which had been specially written for the ensemble, placed the characters at an Australian military airport as they waited for the bodies of their deceased loved ones to arrive back home

Not only did Rabe, like Maddock, prove to be a talented director, but she was the first to know her cast intimately, to know how they liked to work, both as individuals and as a group. Rehearsals for *Citizens* in particular are held up by many in the AC as an example of what could be achieved when the actors were teamed with a director who was familiar with the working method that they themselves had now evolved over time. *Citizens* was an occasion on which both process and product were not only of high quality, but inseparable—the unspoken ideal, if you like, of the AC from the beginning.

Rabe had demonstrated leadership qualities from the outset and, over time, had developed into one of the group's leaders, perhaps even *the* leader. In a different scenario, once this production was finished, she would have been ideally placed to become the artistic director the AC had never had. Why Rabe? In a word, because she's an 'actor's director'. And it was an 'actors company'. The success of her 2009 production of *Elling* for the STC, starring Darren Gilshenan, later confirmed her ability to direct not only with authority, but also sensitivity. In her debut production with the

AC she coaxed astonishing performances from her *Citizens* cast.

This takes us back to the creation of the AC, to the pressure placed on Nevin to hurry it into existence, and the difficulty she had finding someone other than herself to be its artistic director. It is a bizarre irony that Australia enjoys such a rich abundance of acting talent, but such a scarcity of directors up to the task of harnessing and forging that talent into quality work on stage. In Barrie Kosky's view, this is the biggest problem facing Australia's theatre culture, and he wonders whether it has anything to do with our suspicion of authority figures.

If there was a single contradiction built into the original conception of the AC, it was the dichotomy that existed in Nevin herself: an acknowledgement that directors are at once needed, but unwelcome. In her heart, Nevin wanted to treat a company of elite Australian actors to something special and virtually unheard of, a situation in which they would enjoy a degree of control over their own destinies. At the very least, a situation in which their interests would be, if not paramount, then certainly taken into account. They would produce fine work, which would be born in a rehearsal room that was loving and safe, and where every actor's voice would be listened to. This was what Nevin remembers from her time with Rex Cramphorn, and it was the nurturing atmosphere of Cramphorn's process that, in establishing the AC, she sought to re-introduce into Australian theatre-making at its highest level.

If any single director who worked with the AC had the necessary qualities to deliver that unlikely balance, it is Pamela Rabe. She would, of course, have had to withdraw from the ensemble as a performer, but the missing link between actors and management would have been found. It was one more instance of the AC story being dominated by timing, by bad timing. Why, you ask?

The party was almost over. Half-way through rehearsals for the next play, *Gallipoli*, the actors were informed that the new artistic directors were not going to continue with the ensemble in its current form beyond the end of this, its third season. It would be replaced with a radically different model.

If audiences and critics were less enthusiastic about *The Serpent's Teeth* than those working on the production, it can in part be explained by the choice of venue. *The Serpent's Teeth* played in the large-scale Drama Theatre at the Sydney Opera House, not the easiest to work in. Though large in imagination, Keene's work is intimate in scale. Both productions looked beautiful, but what was achieved on stage did not always reach across the footlights. The production was better suited to Wharf One.

Gallipoli:
trench warfare

Gallipoli was another epic production that drew on the resources of NIDA, whose 2008 third-year, graduating students were now called upon to work on a drama-tised narrative, drawn from primary documents, about the most iconic event in Australian military history. Nigel Jamieson is known for highly visual, large-scale works, and many mainstream ticket-buyers, especially those of advancing years with long memories, loved this spectacular work which filled the stage of the huge Sydney Theatre.

The production was physically demanding, as walls were climbed, and massive stage pictures created using the amassed cast. But, for the AC members themelves, the production required a lot more labour than it did acting, as they bellowed primary documents, ran around endlessly backstage, made hasty costume-changes and popped their heads in and out of holes in the stage floor. Some of the younger actors had a ball—to Eden Falk, it was 'inventive, collaborative theatre-making'—but a few of the older ones feared they might join the honoured fallen.

A salutary lesson learned from researching this essay has been discovering the variety of ways in which a single event can be perceived by those involved and those watching it. There is no such thing as objective truth, of course, no single way of seeing. And therein lies the special challenge for a writer whose aim is to establish 'what happened'. There was only one AC show that *every* actor enjoyed being part of, and that just about *everyone* who saw it was also united in admiration: *The Season at Sarsaparilla*. This explains why members of the AC ensemble, including the most recent additions, were looking forward to their next show, especially since it was to be their last. *The War of the Roses* was not only going to be as massive an undertaking as *The Lost Echo*, it would be directed by Benedict Andrews. For many it turned out to be a much more problematic experience than they expected.

The War of the Roses:
a phoenix rises

After another break of four weeks, the STC Actors Company went into rehearsal at the beginning of October 2008 for what was to be the third of their big achievements: more than twenty-hours hours of Shakespearean drama, ranging from the ascendancy of Richard II to the demise of Richard III, with, in between, the stories of the Henries IV, V and VI. Reduced to eight hours' playing time, it was a cut-and-paste on a grand scale. And they had three whole months to rehearse. While I liked the show a lot myself, and others considered it a 'trashing' of Shakespeare's original texts, personal views need to be put to one side so that we pursue to closure themes raised earlier in this essay. It is however ironic, to the point of perversity, that *Roses* not only divided audience opinion as no other AC production had done, it also tested to near breaking-point the bond of trust previously established between the members of the AC and Benedict Andrews.

To meet the challenge of this huge production, Andrews put all sentimentality aside. In the opinion of some who saw the show, a number of actors were treated with what looked like contempt. For example, being forced to stand still or lie under mountains of grey 'ash' for long periods of time for no better reason to than to enhance a stage picture. While Amber McMahon agreed to submit to the endurance of standing, she did pass out more than once during the run of the show.

And despite the size of the production, some of the actors were given very little that you might call special to do. Of course, all were excited to have actors of the calibre of Cate Blanchett and Robert Menzies in the company, but some original AC members were profoundly disappointed to discover how short a time in the spotlight they would ultimately enjoy. Even a senior actor like Peter Carroll ended up with little of substance to do. It is testimony to the commitment of the AC members that they submitted so entirely to Andrews' creative will. As demanding and personally unrewarding as it was for some, there was no overt dissent. Every single actor gave themselves up entirely to the project. They believed in it. And even Dan Spielman said later that he had seen 'an ensemble up there on the stage'.

The production began with a stunning display of concentrated discipline from Cate Blanchett in Act One, Part One as the emotionally insecure, homosexual medieval king (Richard II), and it ended with the free-flowing virtuosity of Pamela Rabe in Act Two, Part Two as the crookback king (Richard III) responsible for the chaos into which Britain's royal line finally descended. In between, we saw many amazing stage pictures framing as many superbly fearless feats of acting.

By way of example, let me mention just two acting highlights, by original AC members, the experienced Brandon Burke as Edward IV and newcomer Eden Falk as Henry VI, both of whom created performances that can only have been achieved as a result of the time and experience accrued since that first day of rehearsals for

Mother Courage. Yet a no less compelling performance was also produced by the relatively inexperienced Ewen Leslie as Hal/Henry V, demonstrating that equally impressive results can be achieved by guests and 'replacement' actors.

Cate Blanchett remembers being daunted by Andrews' demands. Almost all her work as Richard II was composed of extensive soliloquies delivered directly to the audience. She was required to remain almost entirely still—while enduring an hour-long rain (reign?) of gold petals, some landing uncomfortably on her eyelids and on her lips. An actor usually relies on interaction with other actors and physical movement to help remember lines, but here Blanchett was essentially on her own.

Andrews' primary interest as a director is in what actors can do, and he calls on them to people the spaces in the vast, Spartan stage pictures he likes to create. Blanchett found this stimulating, but initially odd, as she was left to her own devices to find 'a human connection', as she put it. It was a case of giving stage reality to abstract suggestions, of 'making the [director's] abstract ask into something tangible.' As audiences readily acknowledged, she succeeded hugely; but she concedes, no less readily, that there were days when she found rehearsals almost too overwhelming. However difficult the process, Blanchett believes working in theatre 'couldn't get any better' than *The War of the Roses*. It was 'an extraordinary time [...] with that group of people. They were all so passionate about it.'

Some of the pain for those in 'thankless' roles derived from the fact that this also happened to be the AC's final show. For many, after so much labour of love and love of labour, at a personal level the project ended in a whimper. This feeling was exacerbated by the fact that the closing night, and the end to the AC's unique artistic journey, took place a long way from home. *The War of the Roses* had been invited to the 2009 Perth International Arts Festival, and after the last performance on 12 March, just under three years after it all 'officially' began, a party or wake was held in a Perth nightclub. Tom Wright and the STC's executive producer flew over; as a member of the cast, the STC's co-artistic director, Cate Blanchett was also present. But it was hardly what could be called an 'after party' on the scale the project deserved.

Wright made a long and heartfelt speech, yet who was there to hear it apart from seven of the original AC members, various replacements and guests who had roles in this last production, and a number of backstage personnel, notably Senior Stage Manager Georgia Gilbert who had been with the project from the beginning. There was no Robyn Nevin: on stage in Melbourne that night, she was only able to send a video farewell. Nor were any of the original dozen who had withdrawn, but who had nonetheless during their time with the ensemble contributed so much.

6

Conclusions

Like one of those mid-twentieth-century circus troupes, the STC Actors Company came to town, pitched its tent, razzle-dazzled, and then one morning it was gone. Like children, some of us are left behind in awe at the feats of strength and virtuosity, the costumes and the glitter, the wild beasts.

In all, the AC produced ten shows; some were physical giants, but all were huge in the demands they made on the actors. Nearly all of them attracted high praise from one or another segment of Sydney's theatre-going population. Several were so good that they will be remembered as high-water marks in the history of Australian theatre.

So why did the AC not survive beyond three years? The initial reason is money. When Andrew Upton and Cate Blanchett had a chance to examine the figures, it was clear that the project as they found it was un-sustainable. 'That wasn't why we changed it,' explains Upton. 'That's why we thought about changing it.'

Blanchett says they also believed that, as incoming artistic directors, it was their duty to ask questions, to pick apart the AC's purpose for being: 'Why an actors company? What is it giving to the company [as a whole]? Is it correctly placed within the company? And what does it mean?' After consultation with Tom Wright and others, Upton and Blanchett decided not to continue with the AC model as it stood—'Even if there was the money,' adds Upton.

Blanchett says that they have nothing but high praise for Nevin's having conceived the project, taken the idea to the state government and ultimately won out. They commend her 'for saying [that] rehearsal time is important [...] and a whole lot of other layers [in theatre-making] beyond the product that are important: things to protect and foster and nurture'. Nevertheless, she adds, '[L]ooking objectively at the model, we [also] thought it was too sacred.'

To many of us on the outside, the AC was effectively 'shut down'. Blanchett finds the phrase a touch pejorative. Maybe. What the new artistic directors certainly did, with two years of funding still available, was look closely at the successes and nonsuccesses of the project thus far, and emerge with a radically different version. Upton and Blanchett prefer to see their changes as reforms, even if that is not how it felt to some of the AC's original members. When the 'new' ensemble, called The Residents, was described—and all the existing members were welcome to pitch for positions—one senior actor turned to one of the twenty-somethings and whispered: 'I don't think I've ever been sacked before so nicely.'

Pamela Rabe is among those who regret what they regard as the AC's premature demise. For her it is unfinished business, though her 'perception' of what took place between May 2006 and March 2009 continues to shift, and is yet to settle in her mind. When asked if she would have accepted the artistic direction of the AC, had it been offered her, Rabe says that would have 'led into a very pragmatic and necessary conversation about ongoing artistic leadership [...], because we really needed someone to look after us, our product and our process'.

* * *

Three core lessons have emerged from writing this essay, lessons that any state theatre company would do well to heed, should it choose to set up an ensemble within a broader company framework.

One: that a theatrical ensemble requires stable artistic leadership. Administrative leadership, however authoritative, is not enough. While a company the size the STC was able to keep their AC on the road, the ride was too bumpy. We know now that a number of land-mines were hit and that there was simply too much collateral damage. Only an artistic director would have had the necessary authority and been close enough to the process to deal with the inevitable questions and problems as they arose. This is not to suggest that 'guest' directors could not be invited in, but that it must be under more closely defined parameters and in keeping the ensemble's over-arching goals.

In Robyn Nevin's defence, there were perhaps too few precedents of her model in our theatre for errors of judgment not to have been made. But it also has to be said that opportunities to evolve and modify were stymied by the original concept's lack of self-reflexivity, which is to say that it lacked the necessary mechanisms either to critique itself or to take onboard criticism from the outside.

Two: that, regardless of budgetary constraints, membership should not be confined to fixed number.

Although in practice the policy of a Holy Twelve was abandoned—within only a few months, in fact—it was maintained as a fundamental principle almost all the way to the end. Only in the last production, *The War the Roses*, was there no attempt to disguise the reality that, in all but name, guests were core participants in the project. Benedict Andrews believes there should have been a much more fluid membership from the beginning. Not only would some of the shows have been better cast, and the ensemble happier; but more good Australian actors might have been involved.

Three: that the intervention of 'outside' management should not be allowed to limit the range or kind of work practices available to the project actors. Voice and movement classes were regularly postponed, or else dispensed with. The idea of the ensemble doing smaller shows, perhaps in repertoire, or 'side experiments' was never seriously addressed. And yet this kind of flexibility might have been advantageous in so many ways, especially as the months rolled on and fatigue set in. A little more rest-time here and there; working with different acting partners for a change; the opportunity to explore 'intimacy' and 'simplicity', qualities which are just as likely to lead to great nights in the theatre as the juggernaut productions for which the AC will be best remembered.

It is telling that the only time the project did downsize in this manner, for the production of *The Serpents Teeth*, two other side projects popped up. There was a financial factor at play here: suddenly the STC found it had the right to call on the AC members to take a week's unpaid leave. Most rested, but others, especially those with little to do in the Daniel Keene plays, seized an unexpected opportunity. Four of the young actors, McMahon, McElhinney, Falk and Mullins, worked on a self-devised piece which they called *The Loft Project*, which ignited their imaginations and they spent many more weeks working on it in their spare time. Then Peter Carroll and Emily Russell worked on a script the STC had commissioned from Adam Grossetti. Both teams made presentations.

In the closing days of writing this essay I asked Pamela Rabe, the AC's 'wolf mother', to look back and try to summarize for me her personal experience of the project. It had been 'the most important and electric experience of my professional life', she said. When I asked Barrie Kosky the same question, this most enthusiastic of theatre artists and gifted of directors replied: 'I had an incredibly vitalized injection of faith and belief in the theatre ... the work I saw the actors do ... pushing themselves ... and the effect on audiences ... on one side the rigour and seeing its effect ... that fabulous alchemical synergy between stage and auditorium. It made me realize why I do it, why I direct.'

The Residents

The new ensemble model that Upton and Blanchett, together with Tom Wright, have devised appears, so far, to be working well. It is less expensive than the previous one, Nathan Rees' NSW State Government having agreed to fund it for another three years. There have been no controversial departures, and no scandals in the media.

Lessons have been learnt. The Residents have an artistic leader, Tom Wright. The troupe is smaller in number, only nine: but their activities lie at the core of the larger STC engine—hence the significance of their name: they are not visitors or celebrity guests, they 'belong'—they live there. And they meet once a week specifically to discuss what they are doing and why.

Though it was not specified that they should be, The Residents are all youngish, in their 20s and 30s. The call was for actors who could 'make their own work' and, perhaps inevitably, it fell on the ears of a younger generation of actors. On the other hand, that the new ensemble reflects a more 'multicultural' Australia in its make-up is deliberate. No less importantly, they are all on the same pay scale.

That they are youthful in spirit and of much the same age has been useful, because there is a training, educational component to The Residents' program. Not only are classes in physical skills locked into the weekly schedule, so too are lessons in dramaturgy and theatre history. This may not have been appropriate, or necessary, for some of the senior AC members, but one aspect of The Residents' duties is to welcome newcomers to the STC—the cast of a new show, say—and to show them around.

Now in its second year, The Residents have produced only one large-scale work for the general public, *Mysteries*, a triptych of dramas based on the English medieval cycle plays. It played in the experimental Wharf 2 late in 2009. Their next will be a production of the *Oresteia*, to open in July 2010.

But they have been busy behind the scenes as well, working on many other projects. At least eleven Australian playwrights have had new work rehearsed and given readings, even limited public showings. Not all this work has been undertaken with an eye to having a future at the STC: Upton and Blanchett believe their well-resourced company has a duty to contribute to Sydney's broader theatre culture. New works by overseas writers have also been explored.

In 2009, The Residents created a fully-fledged production of Dario Fo's *Accidental Death of an Anarchist* under the aegis of the STC Education Program, along with workshops on Brecht and tragedy. Another 'schools' production, of Shakespeare's *Comedy of Errors*, is to open in August 2010. Also in development, says Wright, are three more projects: *Leviathan*, a piece about Sydney's social history, which is being developed by The Residents with actor/director/writer and founder of Zeal Theatre, Stefo Nantsou; *MiniCommissions*, a sequence of short plays by Australian playwrights, funded by the OzCo Emerging Artists scheme; and *Satyricon*, a rock-theatre piece being developed with Tom Wright for production in early 2011.

For those with nostalgic feelings for the original AC, in March 2010—as I write these lines—a production of *VsMacbeth* is in preparation. It is an STC Nextstage production, undertaken in collaboration with The Border Project, of which Amber McMahon is a founding member. Along with Tom Wright leading The Residents, and Cate Blanchett leading the main company with Andrew Upton, McMahon is a tiny thread linking the creative personnel of the two ensembles. Perhaps there will be more.

* * *

Pamela Rabe is not alone. Every actor interviewed for this essay described their time in the AC as one of the most, if not the most, exciting experiences of their careers. Some have found themselves together again, in new rehearsal rooms back in the sausage-factory system of theatre-making. Others working with them in these productions have been taken aback by the shorthand, the trust and shared understanding that AC members enjoy. And meeting up socially with fellow AC artists can be a very emotional experience— '[We're] a bit like returned soldiers,' says one of the Holy Twelve. After living through all those high moments, and the low, and knitting together as a unit in the struggle to survive, the bond between ensemble members is palpably close and heartfelt.

Examined from close up, as this essay has done, the story of the AC is fraught with set-backs and trauma. Seen from the distance of the stalls and in hindsight, however, it is a glitter of fabulous memories.

Readers' Forum

Responses to Robert Walker's *Beethoven of Britney?*, and Brent Salter's *Copyright, Collaboration*

Associate Professor Deirdre Russell-Bowie, who spoke at the Sydney launch of *Beethoven or Britney?*, has researched and taught music education at the University of Western Sydney for more than thirty years.

I should like to respond to Robert Walker's essay by sharing our situation at the University of Western Sydney (UWS).

Despite the fact that research has consistently shown that pre-service teacher education students have little formal music education when they enter their course, face-to-face hours in music education for these students has decreased significantly over the past thirty years, from 68 hours in a three-year undergraduate course in 1980, to just four hours in 2009 in a postgraduate 18-month course. The 24 hours that students receive in the current UWS Creative Arts undergraduate unit is made up of 15% for each discrete art form, then 40% on effective integration of the arts across the curriculum. This content is based on research into teachers' needs in relation to arts education—on the DET and NSW Institute of Teachers' requirements—and from experience and research that indicates that the arts will only be taught if they are integrated into other 'more important' subjects in the primary curriculum.

Research indicates that primary teachers do not teach music because no priority is accorded the subject: they lack resources, confidence in music, training in music and music education, and allocated time in the crowded curriculum. The current M.Teach.(Primary) course ensures that students can download a significant quantity of practical resources online and use the textbook, that they can research the importance of the arts in schools, that they spend at least 20 hours learning and making music to develop their personal confidence in music, and that they participate in practical and theoretical learning experiences in music education and authentic classroom integration.

In NSW there has always been a policy of not having specialists in primary state schools. In 2000, the NSW Creative Arts Syllabus was produced, replacing the music and visual arts syllabuses. The new syllabus described each of four art forms to be taught by generalist teachers. It had fairly generalised separate outcomes, indicators and content for each art form,l and also recommended that teachers interrelate the objectives in each of the art forms as they develop their teaching programs, thus encouraging integration.

Following the recommendations of Professor Ken Eltis's 2003 *Evaluation of Outcomes and Assessment Reporting in NSW Schools*, Foundation Statements for each Key Learning Area (KLA) and each stage were developed. These are descriptions of the knowledge and skills that each student should develop at each stage of primary school and contained one statement per strand/ art form per stage in each KLA. The terms were generic, e.g. Foundation Statement for Kindergarten stipulates that students should 'sing, play and move to a range of music', while the statement for Year 5/6 requires that 'students sing, play and move to a range of music, both as individuals and in a group situation, demonstrating an understanding of musical concepts'.

Connected Outcomes Groups (COGs) were developed for NSW state primary schools in response to the crowded curriculum and in order to ensure that teachers achieve the goals of these Foundation Statements. They offer a systematic integrated approach to covering outcomes and content areas across years and stages in the four KLAs. So far, thirty COGs units have been developed, integrating Human Society and the Environment (HSIE), Science, (Personal Development, Health and Physical Education (PDHPE)) and Creative Arts across all four stages. If all COGs units for that stage are completed in two years (one per term), the Foundation Statements are seen to have been achieved.

However, the Creative Arts are only minimally included—maybe two or three art forms per COG with no depth or development across the years—with the result that students could go through an entire year with very little music. Many public schools are using COGs: the set timeframe for implementation of the COGs is 40% of the week; Maths and English take up 50% and 10% respectively for other activities.

If schools are not doing COGs, they are often teaching to the National Assessment Project for Literacy and Numeracy. One student reported, when he asked to teach a music lesson on his practicum class, that his teacher told him, 'We don't do the Creative Arts, as we are teaching NAPLAN.'

In their *Charter on Primary Schooling*, the Australian Primary Principals' Association designated the four core learning areas of English literacy, mathematics, science and social education to be taught in all Australian primary schools. Other non-core learning areas (including music education) are left to the schools to accommodate, depending on the interest, support, time, resources or expertise to teach them. These, research tells us, are the very reasons why many generalist teachers do NOT teach music!

It is clear that schools in wealthy areas have more music education than those in poorer areas; and in schools where English is a first language for most children, music is taught more often than in schools where there is a high proportion of students from a non-English-speaking background. In the wealthy, mainly English-speaking schools, parents want their children to have a good music education, whereas in many schools situated in low socio-economic-status areas parents do not regard music education as a priority. Thus, lower-economic-status schools following the APPA charter could miss out entirely on music education, if they did not give it the support required. In other words, the question of *Beethoven or Britney?* would be irrelevant.

Professor Walker's paper pointed out that, like the APPA charter, the National Curriculum did not include the arts. However, it has recently been announced that the arts will be included in the National Curriculum, albeit only in the 'second phase'. This is a step, if only a small one, in the right direction.

If the National Curriculum includes the use of specialist teachers in schools, as recommended by the 2005 *National Review of School Music Education*, how might they be used? This is an ongoing debate, with two conflicting arguments, the 'specialist' and the 'generalist'. While the first says that the best music teacher a child could have is a highly-skilled professional artist or performer with relevant training in primary teacher education, the second asserts that the child's best music teacher is the classroom teacher, because s/he knows the children well and can integrate music within the classroom. The children then see music as part of their whole curriculum, not separated from the reality of day-to-day schoolwork.

However, cannot specialist teachers work *with* generalist teachers? A specialist teacher may work as an advisory teacher in a single school, or be shared between several small schools. They could work in a supportive role in the lower grades, where children are in the greatest need of pastoral care and where integration of subjects tends to occur more frequently. In the upper grades they could be used in a semi-replacement role, which would seem appropriate for children of this age-group and could also provide professional development for the classroom teachers. This model has worked well in other states in schools that have specialist music teachers.

If music education continues the way it has been going for many years, we will certainly move beyond the 'state of crisis' that Robert Walker speaks of in his essay—into a state of oblivion. However, if the National Curriculum has any influence on music education in schools, then perhaps we have come to a turning-point in music education. One day we may have to answer his question: *Beethoven or Britney?*

John Weidman is a librettist who has written the books for a wide variety of musicals, among them *Pacific Overtures*, *Assassins*, and *Road Show* with Stephen Sondheim, and *Contact*, created in collaboration with director/choreographer Susan Stroman. For ten years, he served as President of the Dramatists Guild of America.

I read with interest Brent Salter's Platform Paper on *Copyright, Collaboration and the Future of Dramatic Authorship* and, while I agree entirely with his conclusion that the copyright laws should not be changed to accommodate the interests (a better word, I think, than 'rights') of non-writer collaborators, I thought it might be useful to add a few words on a related subject with which we have been wrestling here in the United States.

That issue is director's copyright. Or, more accurately, an aggressive effort by certain directors, through their union, the Society of Directors and Choreographers, to establish a copyright interest in the work which they create—not as putative authors or non-writer collaborators—but simply as directors doing the work they do when they put a play on its feet.

The assertion by these directors that they should own their 'direction' is relatively new. It is, however, deeply dangerous and it is essential that it be resisted, not only by playwrights and other theatre professionals but, frankly, by directors themselves. Why?

Let me begin by emphasizing that in the United States there is no property right, established either by statute or by court decision, which gives a director ownership of any aspect of a theatrical production. Indeed, attempts by directors to copyright their direction is a relatively recent phenomenon, traceable back to the case of *Gutierrez v. DeSantis,* No. 95-1949 (S.D.N.Y. filed 22 March 1995).

The *Gutierrez* case arose out of a production of *The Most Happy Fella,* directed at the Goodspeed Opera House and subsequently on Broadway, by Gerry Gutierrez (a brilliant, accomplished, and celebrated director). Mr Gutierrez attempted to copyright his direction of *The Most Happy Fella* by writing his stage directions in the margins of author Frank Loesser's script and filing those stage directions with the U.S. Copyright Office.

It is important to point out that such a filing is simply that—a filing. It establishes nothing about the ownership of the material filed, nor whether that material is even capable of being owned. And, as already mentioned, there is nothing in the U.S. Copyright Laws, nor has there ever been a judicial determination, to say that stage directions, filed by a director, are copyrightable.

For the sake of argument, however, let's say they are. Let's say that Mr Gutierrez could and did acquire copyright ownership of his staging of *The Most Happy Fella*. What would have been the consequence?

The Most Happy Fella opened on Broadway in 1956. In the forty years between that opening and Mr Gutierrez's revival, there must have been hundreds, if not thousands, of productions of this enormously popular musical play. If Mr Gutierrez could acquire copyright ownership of *his* staging, then the directors of each and every one of these productions could have acquired copyright ownership of theirs as well. And copyright, of course, does not attach to work based on its prominence or quality. The director of a junior high school production of *The Most Happy Fella* in Peoria, Illinois, would be entitled to the same copyright ownership of *her* direction as would Mr Guiterrez.

Had this happened, had the directors of all these productions been able to assert ownership of their direction, what would have been the result? Over the course of the last four decades *The Most Happy Fella* would have gradually ceased to exist as an independent piece of dramatic literature, giving way instead to a multitude of 'Most Happy Fellas', each one a legal partnership between Frank Loesser and a director whose production he and his heirs had, in all likelihood, never even seen.

Should such copyright partnerships ever come into existence, they would clearly operate as liens on plays and musicals, restricting—in unknown and unpredictable ways—the playwright's ability to control and to exploit what he or she has created. But beyond that, they would have a potentially devastating effect on the facility and vitality of theatrical production generally.

For example. Imagine that a theatre wished to produce *The Most Happy Fella*. They would be faced with a choice. They could examine—how?—each of the then existing copyrighted productions and select the one they wished to reproduce. Or they could proceed with their own original production, running the risk that a particular piece of business, or a stage effect, or their overall approach would be attacked by a director as an infringement of his previously copyrighted version.

Of course, *The Most Happy Fella* is merely illustrative.

Even plays which are currently in the public domain, plays which have been freely available to producers and directors and most importantly to the *public* for hundreds of years—*Hamlet, King Lear*—would acquire *de facto* copyrights as more and more directors asserted ownership of *their* versions of these classics. Producing them would become increasingly problematic.

And risky.

Theatres do not want to be sued. Indeed, most of them cannot afford the expense of defending a lawsuit. And if directors were able to copyright their work, the day would inevitably come when a theatre decided to cancel a production simply because they had been threatened by a director who perceived—rightly or wrongly—that the theatre's production would infringe on a version which belonged to him.

Infringement, of course, requires copying. And copying requires access. But directors are not attorneys, they are artists. And there are plenty of artists—and, I assure you, I am not exempting playwrights—who are prone to see their influence in other people's entirely original work. It is not difficult to initiate a lawsuit. It is even less difficult to write a letter threatening one. And the impact of such threats on theatrical production could be potentially paralyzing.

A recent, hopeful development. In the context of another law suit provoked by his union, John Rando, the award-winning director of the 2001 Broadway production of the musical *Urinetown*, made several attempts to register his direction with the U.S. Copyright Office. All of his attempts were rejected. Indeed, the Copyright Office took the position that direction, as a matter of law, is not copyrightable. And in an unprecedented move, the Copyright Office asked the Department of Justice to intervene in the *Urinetown* case on behalf of the position it had taken.

As it happened, the *Urinetown* case was settled before it went to trial, so the position of the Copyright Office was never memorialized in a judge's decision. Still, one can only hope that the unequivocal position which it took will cause other directors to think twice before attempting to assert copyright ownership of the work which they create.

It is a cliché to say that Americans live in a litigious society. This does not make it any less true. Or demoralizing. Or dangerous. Dangerous in this case, because if only one director one day finds himself before a judge sympathetic to the idea that he should own his direction, the crippling effect on the theatre could be enormous, and the resulting mischief could take years to sort out.

Wayne Harrison is the director of three current or forthcoming productions: Don Reid's *Codgers*, Andy Griffiths' *Just Macbeth* and Alex Buzo's *Macquarie.*

Reading Brent Salter's recent Platform Paper, *Copyright, Collaboration* I was taken by Tom Wright's recollection of the 1980s as a time when directorial 'ownership' became a contested issue, when 'directors saw themselves as the primary auteur voice and came to seek to impose their own reading on texts and productions' (p.33) and how this occasionally caused conflict. In the early '80s, when I first became involved in dramaturgy and the creation of new work for the mainstage, the orthodoxy was that theatre was a writer's medium. And while you could sometimes encounter a disgruntled director, revealing that such-and-such a play was a mess until 'I'd knocked it into shape', the orthodoxy—the primacy of the author—held. Except, as I worked further into the mainstream and became a director myself, I could discern a parallel theatre practice that *didn't* uphold the orthodoxy at all. And people were writing about this.

In an *Aspect* article entitled 'Where Things Begin' the author discusses the influence of Antonin Artaud on practitioners such as Brook, Bausch and Grotowski. He goes on to decipher what *The Theatre and Its Double* was advocating and how this might influence contemporary theatre:

> [T]he central character in Artaud's conception of theatre is the director, who is to have both the practical and theoretical intelligence of his subject. [...T]he author is the one who possesses the language of words. But this monarchic and rather stifling conception loses its pertinence from the moment a new syntax of lights, music, colours and gestures becomes available again.

This article was written by Jacques Delaruelle, back in 1985. Now, as Tom Wright also suggests in *Copyright, Collaboration*, there is a new generation of theatre writers, not necessarily designating themselves as playwrights, who are prepared to hitch their talents to a director's vision, or at least to the creation of something bigger than the writer, a theatrical production—those whom Ben Winspear describes as having 'a younger appreciation of text [...], more varied and more open to interaction' (p.13). And this, I would suggest, is what underlay the media skirmish last year between David Williamson and Barrie Kosky: what was once orthodox is now old-fashioned or, at least, out of fashion, or worse, tainted by spokesmen like the version of Edward Albee presented in *Copyright, Collaboration*: egomaniacally stupid, claiming that only the Word can bring about an 'engagement of thought', denying directors and designers the right to creativity and suggesting that 'they go fuck themselves'.

Well, they choose not to do this, but instead, to run theatre companies that include writers, but do not idolize them. This is perhaps best illustrated by the Melbourne example, where the playwright-driven Playbox Theatre Company, once the impervious citadel of Australian playwriting was swept away, to be replaced by the theatre-maker-inspired Malthouse with Michael Kantor at the helm. Michael was a performer in Kosky's Gilgul Theatre Company in the early 1990s and is known affectionately as one of the 'Kosky Kinder'—which is not to deny him his own identity as a fine director's theatre director.

Inevitably, the new fashion for collaborative theatre-making will affect the carving up of royalties and it can't be hidden behind the rather feeble defence offered in *Copyright, Collaboration*, namely that courts and judges prefer the simplicity of dealing with one royalty holder and that the legal framework is used 'to minimize the number of original-authorial contributions'. There are too many precedents for this to hold.

When a play is adapted from another source, there is often a dual or allocated royalty: to the adapter, such-and-such a percentage; to the writer of the original novel, the complement. No doubt it would be neater for the legal eagles if these rights holders could be minimized to a sole author. But that would not reflect the truth of the creation. What's wrong with the following arrangement? To the author(s) of the play, such-and-such a percentage; to the author(s) of the production, the complement, if this is a truthful reflection of the way in which the 'piece of theatre' has been created. Surely, our courts aren't too lazy to acknowledge and action this? And we wouldn't want our royalty system to be based on lies, would we? When the title-page of a published text reads 'by Joe (or Joan) Blogg', we want to believe that what follows is all his or her own work. I've been to too many dinners with disgruntled directors, where the wine has flowed, not to know that this has far too often been simply not the case. The law should not protect those who are prepared to pass off other people's work as their own, and as Brent Salter indicates, industry-based contracting practices are being varied and tailored to reflect this.

Ultimately, authorship can't reside, as Alana Valentine contends, with the person 'who types up the scene at the end of the day' (p.12). That may hint at ownership, but not authorship. If it were so, in many projects the owners would end up being the stage managers, keeping track of the changes made in the rehearsal room and writing them up in the prompt copy at the end of the day.

My experience of royalty allocation can be summed up as follows: it all depends on your grunt and leverage. Trevor Nunn got the credit for writing several lines of 'Memory', the hit song from Andrew Lloyd Webber's musical *Cats*, because he *was* Trevor Nunn, the world's most sought-after director of musicals. His grunt earned him millions of pounds in royalties, which must have been a bastard for lawyers to administer. If Sir Trevor had been working in the Australian theatre industry when he wrote those lines, he would have been obliged to sign away the rights to his lyrical contribution—to Lord Lloyd Webber, who, having typed it up at the end of the day (or collected it from the stage manager), would have been within his legal right to claim sole authorship. Sir Trevor's only recourse would have been to inflate his director's fee so as to include a buy-out of all authorial contributions and any exploitation of subsequent productions (in any media) and subsidiary rights, everything from musical greeting-cards to karaoke tracks.

But, of course, you would need a crystal ball to predict what the inflation should be. Where originating producer's royalties are concerned, I've always believed that these should not be a 'best intentions' additional royalty that exists outside of the authorial royalty, but guaranteed points that are legally coupled to the author's royalty, or else a percentage of the latter automatically paid by the author to the original producer. This royalty can be capped to an amount equivalent to the original investment, or waived until a certain level of income is achieved. Waiver, full or conditional, is a way to modify royalty packages and works better than the wimpy 'best endeavours'. Few playwrights and agents have the grunt or the political will to enforce originator royalties.

But waivers are sometimes treated with suspicion in the light of cases such as *Strictly Ballroom*, in which several organizations involved in the original stage versions of the work (NIDA, STC) were asked to waive any residual hold they might have over the property so that the film version could be made. They did as requested, the film was made and it became a substantial commercial success. Someone made a lot of money out of it, but not the organizations that had produced it originally.

Which is to answer Alana Valentine, who asks why an artistic director 'who has a full-time job' (p.18) would be interested in copyright and the future exploitation of work? Originating royalties that flow to grant-assisted companies do not serve to line the pockets of individuals working for those companies, but, ideally, to enable the companies to continue producing original work, i.e. to create, we hope, more *Strictly Ballrooms*.

As to the future, theatrical fashion is a strange thing. Coward, Rattigan, Priestley were all swept away in the 1950s, once John Osborne's kitchen-sink realism took the English stage by storm, but one by one these idols of a previous era had their careers revived, their reputations restored. Priestley has been a particular beneficiary: the 'director's-theatre number' that Stephen Daldry did on it turned *An Inspector Calls* into an international, commercial hit that is still running in London fifteen years later. It would be interesting to see the allocation of *those* royalties. It may be that an Artaud-inspired director's theatre, or one of another kind, is merely a phase through which we shall pass and the pendulum will swing back etc etc. After all, the era into which we are entering here in Sydney is one in which none of the key grant-assisted companies, STC, Belvoir or Griffin, is run by a director, but rather by an actor, writer, designer and dramaturg.

Subscribe to **Platform Papers**

Have the papers delivered quarterly to your door

4 issues for $60.00 including postage within Australia

The individual recommended retail price is $14.95.

___ I would like to subscribe to 4 issues of Platform Papers for $60.00

I would like my subscription to start from: ___ this issue (No. 23)

___ the next issue (No. 24)

Name_____

Address_____

_____

_____ State _____ Postcode _____

Email _____

Telephone _____

Please make cheques payable to Currency House Inc.

Or charge: ___ Mastercard ___ Visa

Card no. ___ ___ ___ ___ ___ ___ ___ ___ ___ ___ ___

___ ___ ___ ___

Expiry date _____ Signature _____

Fax this form to Currency House Inc. at: 02 9319 3649

Or post to: Currency House Inc., PO Box 2270,
Strawberry Hills NSW 2012 Australia